THE MAN WHO WON

Writer Andy Devlin's debts spiral out of control and he's forced to sell his home to pay them off. Andy finds himself unable to afford a new place to live. By a quirk of fate, calamity strikes his two closest friends and, for the first time, the three friends are split up. Brad has a dramatic change of fortune and sets about buying a luxurious home in the country for a neighbourly reunion. But his act of generosity will create more problems than it solves . . .

GUY BELLAMY

THE MAN WHO WON

Complete and Unabridged

ULVERSCROFT
Leicester

First published in Great Britain in 2005 by
Robert Hale Limited
London

First Large Print Edition
published 2006
by arrangement with
Robert Hale Limited
London

British Library CIP Data

Bellamy, Guy, *1935* –
    The man who won.—Large print ed.—
    Ulverscroft large print series: general fiction
    1. Male friendship—Fiction 2. Finance, Personal—
    Fiction 3. Large type books
    I. Title
    823.9′14 [F]

    ISBN 1–84617–208–x

Published by
F. A. Thorpe (Publishing)
Anstey, Leicestershire

Set by Words & Graphics Ltd.
Anstey, Leicestershire
Printed and bound in Great Britain by
T. J. International Ltd., Padstow, Cornwall

This book is printed on acid-free paper

For Jean Parratt MBE

1

After he had read his post, Andy Devlin wondered whether to put a bullet in his brain, but dismissed the idea almost immediately on the reasonable grounds that he didn't own a gun and wouldn't know how to use it if he did. He was not a practical man. Instead, he found a bottle of red wine, a couple of glasses and a book and went out to the doubtful pleasures of his back garden, where he sank into a very old deckchair and stared vacantly at the hydrangeas. He had always intended to get a comfortable sunbed for these occasional escapes from his tiny office upstairs but could never afford the garden centre's prices. He couldn't afford wine either, but this vino de mesa from Valencia, discovered on the bottom shelf of the supermarket with a screw top instead of a cork, cost less than two pounds.

His depression would have been eased by a phone call to one of his friends, Clive or Brad, inviting them round to share this cheap plonk, but the phone was in the process of being cut off. The cutting off had reached an intermediate stage in which he was allowed to receive calls but not make them. This was intended to encourage him to write a cheque, a venture in which the discouragement of the bank was a far more potent force than the hopeful urging of the telephone company.

The post that had reduced him to despair today had arrived in many envelopes but each carried the same implacable message. The local council were desperate for money, the electricity board craved it, the water people were stunned by its non-appearance. The Inland Revenue, who had conjured a fanciful figure out of thin air on the basis of a cheque he had received three years ago, were turning nasty, and the phone people had already moved in. Three credit cards, one of them attached to a popular store, were advancing on him like camouflaged paratroopers with a grenade in each hand. (The credit cards had long been removed from his own armoury, but the debts were still there.)

Letters which once suggested mildly that a prompt payment would be appreciated had now assumed a more menacing tone. Some no longer even arrived from the creditors, but came instead from specialist solicitors, hired guns who had been employed to separate the quarry from his loot. To this end, quite regardless of the fact that the quarry had no loot, they used language designed to intimidate, and Andy Devlin had to admit that he was thoroughly intimidated. From today's post he could already recite verbatim quotations from three of his bemused creditors, each at different stages of their assault.

1. If this amount is not paid within ten days, solicitors will be instructed to issue legal proceedings against you.

2. Our clients are now aware that you have failed to comply with our arrangement, and we are therefore proceeding with legal action, applying the costs directly to your account.

3. A liability order for the sum of £560 was issued against you by the magistrates' court in respect of non-payment of council tax.

But this little debt mountain wasn't the worst of it. Far more ominous was the looming presence of the bank, who in brighter and more promising days had been persuaded to lend him a five-figure sum 'to tide him over'. All they wanted in exchange for this unbridled generosity were the deeds to his house.

The nest egg, rapturously received and celebrated with champagne, shrunk alarmingly when no other money arrived to join it, and now he was left with enough to run their small family car and buy food, but not to settle the larger debts that dominated that day's mail.

The twenty-first century was developing a bleak and hostile air that he didn't like.

He poured himself some wine and opened his book. It was a history of Elizabethan England, which helped him get today into perspective. The wine helped in other directions. After a few glasses he was occasionally suffused by an optimism that verged on the irrational so that he could blissfully ignore the fact that a tidal wave of debt would soon sweep him out of his house and into the street.

He was thirty-nine and felt ten years younger. If it wasn't for the knee injury, he would still be playing Sunday-morning football in the park with Clive and Brad. But with his short, blond hair and slim figure he still looked like a sportsman, he told himself. At one time, after a trial at Watford, a career as a professional footballer had seemed a real possibility, but this prospect, like several others, had been blown away by the malign forces of fate.

The garden in which he was sitting had little to commend it; gardening was not one of his interests. There was a small patio, a neat lawn that he regularly mowed, and a child's swing, no longer used. The highlight was in one corner where Clare, seduced by a dozen television programmes, had created a vine-entwined pergola, adorned by garlands of honeysuckle. Her favourite pale mauve hydrangeas swamped the surrounding borders. In this rustic setting, he discovered, the book and the wine made conflicting demands: the book required concentration which the wine dissipated.

The contest was swiftly resolved, however, when Clare appeared round the side of their detached three-bedroom house. He looked up as she sauntered sexily across the lawn and lowered herself into the second deck-chair. She had short black hair and a round, pretty face with eyes that sparkled — although the sparkle had faded a little in recent months.

'Where's Greg?' he asked.

She had been to pick up their ten-year-old son from school.

'Indoors, doing his homework. I think our poverty is really motivating him.'

Andy found this hard to believe and thought it more likely that their errant son was wrestling with the challenge of Ridge Racer Revolution on his PlayStation.

Clare leaned back in her chair and sighed. 'I know you come into this world with nothing, and leave with nothing, but aren't you supposed to have something in between?'

Andy groped hopelessly for a reassuring reply. He was full of admiration for the stoical way his wife endured their money problems, never harping on about the clothes she couldn't buy, or the holidays they couldn't afford. He looked at her short skirt and tight sweater and reflected that at one time in this situation an eruption of carnal fervour would have had them sprawling on the grass. But money did funny things to the libido and when he looked at her now he saw only debts.

He held up the book he was reading. 'Hey, when Walter Raleigh was beheaded, his wife carried his embalmed head around with her for the rest of her life. Would you do that for me?'

'Probably not.'

'You can't get the loyalty these days.'

She turned to look at the book he was reading. 'They don't behead people these days, do they?'

'Not at the moment,' he conceded. 'Not right now — but you never know which way this government's going to swerve.'

She leaned back and closed her eyes. 'Anyway, darling,' she said in a more businesslike tone, 'what are you writing at the moment? What huge effort has sent you exhausted into the garden with a bottle of wine?'

It was a difficult question. What *was* he writing now? He called himself a writer, so he had to be writing something. Writers never stopped — it was a kind of sickness. The job itself wasn't very complicated; it only involved covering sheets of paper with words. Children did it. You didn't need expensive equipment. A pad and a pen and you were in business — or not, as the case may be.

In the panic that gripped him now he had lurched from one project to another, unsure which might yield the jackpot he needed. For some years he had written a column for a monthly magazine, which took a wry look at current events, but the magazine had folded, the way magazines do, and there had been no clamour from the surviving rivals to inherit his lugubrious maunderings. The absence of amusing sitcoms on television had seemed to provide a suitable case for his attention, but his jokes developed a humourless quality within the restrictions of a thirty-minute script and even he couldn't smile. For a time he reviewed films for an obscure avant-garde magazine that was published in the Midlands, but the cheque produced by his insightful verdicts barely covered the cost of his trips to the various cinemas. He moved on to comic verse.

In his formative years, when the knee injury put paid to football and laid him up for two months, he had written a novel about the callous promiscuities of youth. It had been published and praised, but when he tried to write a second one he discovered the truth of the saying that everybody has one novel in them. He had written his.

It was the novel that set him off on this scribbling business in the first place, but today it seemed as if everybody was scribbling. There were more people writing than reading.

So what was he writing now? He supposed, if you counted up the hours that he had devoted to it, that he was writing a play — a play about Sir Walter Raleigh that would, he assured himself in his darkest moments, start life on the chilly boards of a West End theatre before being triumphantly transferred to the lavish setting of a Hollywood studio where world-famous stars would grovel obsequiously for the starring roles.

A play about Walter Raleigh? Writing it was like pushing water uphill.

He declared neutrally: 'I'm writing a play.'

But he was spared the good-natured derision this might have invited by the sudden appearance on the lawn of Clive Preston.

'Greg told me you were both out here,' he said, looking gaunt. He was a tall, thin man, a year older than Andy, and he always dressed immaculately in dark grey suits. The tie might be vanishing from a thousand offices, but its survival was assured in the staid surroundings where Clive pursued his successful career. He was the business development and marketing manager of a big cosmetic concern whose inventive products — cleaning, curing and beautifying the loyal customers — reached the farthest corners of the globe.

Clare stood up.

'Take this seat, Clive,' she said. 'I've got to get dinner. You're welcome to stay, but I doubt whether corned beef and mashed potatoes holds much appeal.'

'Thank you, Clare,' he said, folding his lanky frame into the ancient chair. 'I'll pass on the dinner. I'm on my way home to have a serious talk with Holly.'

'Not too serious, I hope?' said Clare with a little laugh.

'Pretty bloody serious,' Clive grunted, and waited until she had gone before turning to Andy.

'Can you get hemlock in Boots?' he asked.

'Hemlock?'

'It seemed to do a number on old Socrates.'

Andy studied his visitor, unsure where this was leading. Playing in the same amateur football team as Clive and Brad had, for some indiscernible reason, provided their friendship with an almost psychic bond that had held them together ever since as if they had fought in the same trench at the Somme. Even their homes were within a hundred yards of each other. The pressures of a demanding job had aged Clive more than his friends. The thin hair had receded and was flecked with grey. The man who had once been a loping centre-half, when they had such a position, no longer had the same energy levels.

'You're not the suicidal type, Clive. You're the get-up-and-go type. That's why you earn so much money.'

'That isn't true, unfortunately,' Clive replied dismally. 'If I hadn't had the option of suicide, I'd have killed myself long ago. Anyway, I don't earn a lot of money. In fact, I don't earn any money.'

'You've turned amateur?'

'I've been sacked.'

Andy reached for the wine bottle and the spare glass he had brought out for Clare. 'You'd better have some of this then.' He watched while his friend took a swig: it wasn't the sort of wine that Clive was accustomed to drinking. 'What do you think of it?' he asked.

Clive politely took another sip. 'All right to gargle with, I suppose,' he said. 'Where's it from?'

'Spain. Valencia.'

'They make better.'

'Better costs more,' said Andy. 'You'll get used to it.'

'I may have to.'

'So what happened?'

Clive took another tentative sip and put the glass down. 'I made a fool of myself, I'm afraid. They were quite right to sack me, no question.'

'Made a fool of yourself? That doesn't sound like you.'

'I was drugged.'

Embarrassed by this confession, he picked up the glass and emptied it. 'Have you got any more of this? It's quite acceptable once you get over the initial shock.'

Andy got up and went back into the house in search of his last remaining bottle. Clare, sitting on a high stool, was peeling potatoes in the kitchen.

'He wants more of that?' she said. 'I'm amazed. I didn't think he would touch it.'

'He's been sacked,' Andy told her. 'He's distraught.'

'Sacked? What for?'

'I'm about to find out.'

He carried the bottle out to the garden, where a sinking sun was beginning to throw shadows across the lawn. Clive sat motionless in his chair, evidently deep in thought, and didn't move when Andy returned to his seat.

Eventually he stirred. 'Did you know that desperation is an anagram of 'a rope ends it'?' he asked.

Andy unscrewed the bottle and poured them both a drink. 'Keep taking the wine,' he said. 'You can feel quite optimistic after about three bottles, if you're still conscious.'

But Clive was now gazing distractedly around the garden. 'That's a fine pergola Clare's made. Your wife's a clever woman.'

'The only mistake she made was marrying me.'

Clive came alive at this to wave an admonitory finger. 'Don't put yourself down, Andrew. You just haven't had much luck.'

'I've had a lot of luck but it's all been bad. Are you going to tell me why you were drugged and sacked?'

Clive now covered his eyes with one hand. 'I can hardly bear to talk about it,' he groaned.

'Have a go.'

The sun dipped another inch and the

temperature dropped with it. The garden was no longer the warmest place to be, and Clive, realizing this, decided to talk while they still had their privacy. He pulled himself up in his seat and drank some more wine.

'I had an idea after lunch,' he said. 'When I got home I'd give Holly a pleasant surprise.'

'That's nice,' said Andy. 'She deserves it.'

'The thing was that one of the chaps had bought some Viagra during the lunch break.'

'You don't need Viagra.'

'No, I don't, but I was curious about what it did.'

'So you took some?'

'A pretty hefty dose, actually. What I didn't realize was the timescale attached to this particular ingestion. I'd taken it about four hours too early and . . . well, it's terrible to admit it, but I ended up shagging the cleaning lady.'

'The cleaning lady?'

'On my desk.'

'Terrific,' said Andy. He didn't know whether to laugh or frown.

'The desk was the second mistake. If I'd done it on the floor nobody would have seen.'

'People saw you?'

'Dozens of them, apparently. I got a round of applause at the end.'

Andy drank some wine. The picture that

Clive's story evoked was difficult to take seriously. But his friend was taking it very seriously. He looked desolate.

'And the cleaning lady? How did she react to this interruption in her busy schedule?'

'She was very grateful, as it happens. Single mum of thirty-two. She was up for it. However, my boss took a different view.'

'What did he say?'

'Goodbye, basically. I was out of the door within the hour. That's why I'm home early. That's why I had time to drop in on you.' He turned in his chair and looked at Andy. 'What the hell am I going to tell Holly?'

'That you've been sacked? Office politics? Jealous rivals? Incompetent management? Unfair dismissal?'

'The problem there is that she'll expect me to go to arbitration. I haven't a case to put to those po-faced bunglers, have I?'

'Not a very good one,' Andy admitted. 'Bonking the hired help wasn't part of your job description. The panel would spot that.'

They sat in silence, considering the dilemma.

'I think what I might do,' Clive said after a while, 'is go round after dinner to see Brad. He's got ideas.'

'He's got money.'

'He might even have a job.'

14

'I'll come with you,' Andy said, 'just as soon as I've sampled the culinary delights of corned beef.'

2

They were greeted at the door by that most ominous of questions: 'Have you heard the news?' It came from Brad's wife, Olivia, a willowy blonde with hazel eyes and a small pursed mouth, who stood pale-faced on the threshold, searching their faces for an answer. They stared back at her blankly and shook their heads, fearful about what they were going to be told. 'You'd better come in,' she said, standing reluctantly to one side.

When they walked up the road to Brad's little mansion, with its five bedrooms, large lawned garden, new clay tennis court and small swimming pool tucked into a large green conservatory, they had imagined that a bright interlude was about to compensate for a disastrous day.

Clive, who had managed to reveal his new jobless existence to his wife without actually telling her the true reason for this change in his situation, nurtured hopes that their host would in some way have the solution to his problem.

Brad, the third member of their triumvirate, was a big bear of a man, the goalkeeper in their old football team, who had a lot of unruly black curly hair that made him look like a mad conductor who spent his life in conflict with recalcitrant violinists. Ambition, energy and cunning had driven him to create his own public relations agency, Bradley Rowe Images, which was installed in elegant offices high over the West End. It was a method of earning a living which he liked to describe as 'lying for money'. He explained how a positive veneer could be laid over the most dismal of subjects. A rapist? Sexy, virile, strong. A killer? Adventurous, fearless, proficient. In a world of half-truths, his perceptive employees knew which half to ignore and which half to praise and promote.

But this evening, as Olivia led them through the house to the conservatory where Brad was sitting motionless but far from relaxed on a rattan sofa, Andy and Clive could see that they had gatecrashed a wake. Brad's body language was simple to read. His hands, normally so busy in lifting drinks, igniting cigars, or just gesticulating vividly to augment his spiel, lay face down on his knees in a curiously defeated gesture. The flesh around his eyes suggested that tears had been shed.

Andy's first thought was that he had been given a death sentence by his doctor, but

Brad disabused him of this idea almost immediately.

'The light at the end of the tunnel has been switched off,' he pronounced sonorously. 'The bank has waved the chequered flag.'

Clive needed this to be spelt out, 'Do you mean the agency has collapsed?'

'Bludgeoned to death by the money men, to be precise,' Brad said, staring at the floor.

Andy found this almost impossible to believe. Brad was the strongest, the most ruthless of the three of them, the only one to have set out to build his own empire. The proof of his success was all round them. He knew that Bradley Rowe Images was sailing through stormy times. There was another mini-recession which seemed to hit Brad's type of business quicker than most, and the firm had been weakened by the loss of its most accomplished practitioner, a man so adept at mendacity that he had been poached by the government's spin office and now worked in Downing Street. But for it all to have crashed so suddenly was a huge shock. He looked across at Olivia, who was watching this mournful scene. Clive had once described her as a bulimic airhead, but Andy thought she was smarter than that. She had mastered the art of spending Brad's money very quickly and with her Prada dresses and

Farhi suits had a wardrobe full of labels. Today she was wearing an expensive black trouser suit with a colourful striped belt. The arrival of money had produced, after an apparently impoverished childhood, an unwelcome snobbishness, and Andy wondered how she would handle this blow to her status. But her next remark suggested that she would be in there fighting.

'You'll start something else, Brad,' she said in her sexy, husky voice. 'What you've done once you can do twice.'

Brad looked at the others with an expression of deepest despair. 'My wife is a great woman for urging people on. If she saw a gypsy baking a hedgehog she'd tell him that he ought to open a restaurant.'

Olivia ignored this remark and turned to the guests. 'Do you gentlemen want a drink?' she asked.

'Does the Pope wear a funny hat?' said Clive, slumping into a rattan seat which matched the sofa. He was so preoccupied with his own misfortune that he found it difficult to lend Brad the sympathetic ear he needed. One ill-advised taste of Viagra had lost him his job and his income. It was not something that had ever happened to him and he had a new and frightening feeling of insecurity. The help he hoped might have come from Brad would clearly not now appear unless he was going to do a phoenix performance from the ashes — these days firms went bust and reappeared a week later under a new name in the office next door.

'I couldn't believe what Mahatma Coat was telling me,' Brad was saying. Mahatma Coat was evidently the name they had given their Indian accountant. 'The account was closed from 2.31.'

'Are there no assets?' Andy asked.

Brad continued staring at the floor. 'Resale value of the office furniture, I expect. The bank will want the computers to sell off cheap themselves.'

'Well, let me cheer you up, Brad,' said Clive. 'You're not the only one round here who lost his job today. Let me take you away from your disaster, and enthral you with mine.'

Clive's story, possessing a particle of humour that Brad's conspicuously lacked, did bring a smile to their host's face, but when he saw Clive's miserable expression he let it fade.

'And you, Andy?' Brad asked, turning only marginally in his chair. 'Wonderful day?'

'Angry creditors, court orders, solicitors' threats. The usual thing.'

Awe-struck by their collective ill-luck, the

three men fell into a silence that was not broken until Olivia returned. She carried a tray on which stood a bottle of champagne, some fruit juices and various glasses.

'If we're going to say goodbye to affluence we've got to do it properly,' she said. 'I'm serving Bellinis.' Nobody knew what a Bellini was but Olivia was an efficient hostess who couldn't serve you coffee without checking whether you wanted Colombian, Kenyan or Costa Rican. She opened the champagne professionally, without a pop, and explained that you did it by turning the cork and not the bottle.

Bellini turned out to be champagne with peach juice, an exotic mixture that Brad regarded with misgiving.

'I used to drink beer,' he said. 'I liked beer.'

'He used to go out for a quiet drink and come back four days later with one shoe and a beard,' said Olivia. 'We put a stop to that, didn't we, dear?'

'We did, didn't you?' Brad replied sadly.

'You nearly had a drink problem.'

'I still have a drink problem — I've got two hands and only one mouth.'

Andy could well remember the hours the three of them had spent in warm and friendly public houses while the precious gift of time slipped through their fingers. Usually these sessions followed one of their football matches, and although some serious discussions accompanied the drinking — money-making ideas being scribbled on the backs of envelopes to see whether they would survive sober scrutiny later — it all seemed in retrospect to have been time wasted. Brad's startling prosperity only arrived when the single-minded Olivia emerged to wean him off the sherbet.

Hauling himself back to the present, Andy told the others: 'I'm going to lose my house.'

Brad turned to him, looking shocked. 'Surely not?'

'Oh yes. The bank hold the deeds. They'll insist. It's the only way I'm going to clear the debt mountain.'

'What does Clare say?' Olivia asked.

'She's being very good about it.'

Clive, who had got up to admire the small, sparkling swimming pool, wandered back to join them. 'I'll certainly be selling mine,' he said. 'I have a big mortgage tied to a big salary.'

Olivia looked at Brad. 'Have I missed something?' she asked.

'Yes. Clive's lost his job as well,' her husband told her. He didn't feel like revealing the lurid circumstances which precipitated this unexpected journey into unemployment:

whatever sympathy Olivia might be capable of offering would probably evaporate if she had to conjure up visions of a cleaning lady sprawled knickerless on an office desk.

'What a trio you are,' she said, showing no sympathy at all. And then a thought occurred to her. 'Are we going to lose our house, Brad?'

The suggestion seemed to bring Brad back to life. 'No way,' he growled with a flash of the ruthlessness and determination that had helped him to create his agency. 'I'll think of something.'

★   ★   ★

When his friends had left to reshuffle the broken pieces of their lives, Brad made a phone call. It was, like all his calls, brisk and efficient. Two hours later he was driving west. It was one o'clock in the morning.

The shortage of traffic at this time of night allowed him to break all limits and within an hour he had skirted Salisbury and was heading south into deepest Dorset. His Bentley Turbo R, an extravagant purchase at the height of his success, enjoyed speed despite its age. Its agreed value insurance figure was £30,000 but Brad doubted whether he would get half that if he tried to sell it. There had been too many bumps and scrapes, along with the envious damage inflicted by youths with coins in car parks.

He drove on into Hardy country. On a sunny day it would have been a beautiful journey between tree-lined undulating hills, but tonight he could only see the road. His thoughts turned to Andy and Clive, now no doubt contemplating their respective misfortunes, and an unwelcome idea loomed: they were both going to move. This was not something that Brad wanted to happen. They were his two oldest friends and he depended on their company more than he would ever admit to either of them. They represented a solid base in a hard-nosed world of shifting allegiances.

It was one more source of depression in a life that was suddenly full of them, and he reached the farm in a sombre mood. Jeremy, a tall, dark-haired man slightly younger than Brad, came round the side of the house to greet him. He was wearing jeans and boots and a thick black sweater.

'Hallo, cousin,' he said. 'It would take a thousand pounds to keep me out of bed these days.'

'Where's the thing?' Brad asked.

'I've made a start. Follow me.'

The two men walked through a gate and

then trudged across a muddy field towards a strange yellow contraption that stood in the middle of it like a spacecraft at rest on the moon.

'What does JCB stand for, anyway?' Brad asked.

'It was invented by Joseph Cyril Bamford. It's a wonderful toy. I use it to rip out hedges, dig ditches, lay water pipes. I've even moved trees with it because you can take the soil with the root.'

'Get digging,' said Brad.

Jeremy climbed on to the digger while Brad watched. It was a machine that worked at both ends. The back hoe digger dug out the earth, and the bucket at the front lifted it out, a ton at a time. While this was going on, hydraulic jacks were lowered so that all four wheels were off the ground.

It was obvious that Jeremy had made more than a start. He had dug an impressive hole that was ten yards long and nearly six feet deep, but he kept on digging while Brad watched. The expertise of other people never failed to impress him; his cousin was dyslexic, but had far more talents than Brad, and owned many more acres. Eventually he climbed down from his uncomfortable seat and said, 'Go and get it.'

Brad made his way back across the field,

wondering when he had ever felt so miserable. On top of the various causes of his misery, he was tired and cold. He climbed into his Bentley, which he had once loved with a passion, and drove it through the gate and across the field. Jeremy, in the manner of a traffic policeman, directed him to an area at the edge of his newly dug hole.

'I've left a slope,' he said. 'You can drive it in.'

The car bounced down into the hole and Brad climbed out, taking the keys with him. Jeremy was already back up in his seat, and soon loads of earth were being dropped on the car's roof.

An hour later, when he was satisfied that the field looked exactly as it had a few hours earlier, he retracted the hydraulic jacks and put the digger back on its wheels. He turned the machine and drove towards the gate. Brad followed on foot, remembering too late the cherished tapes he had left in the car.

'I seem to recall that part of my fee was for giving you a lift home,' Jeremy said. 'Does Olivia know you are here?'

'Good God, no,' said Brad, flinching at the thought. 'We've had a rather stressful day and she had to take one of her powerful sleeping pills.'

3

Clive Preston was a sensitive man and he realized in a matter of days that he had been effectively demoted in the family hierarchy. Now that the business development and marketing manager in a Gucci suit had metamorphosed into an out-of-work loafer in jeans, different signals were reaching him from his wife and daughter. He had never expected respect at home, but the amiable tolerance he had settled for was now replaced by harsher treatment. Caustic remarks drifted in his direction, withering comments about him were made for no reason, and sarcasm crept into conversations that had once been placid and friendly. He listened to it all with a sinking heart. His place in the general scheme of things had been subjected to a scathing reappraisal.

Holly, the pretty blonde wife who had been by his side for sixteen peaceful years with barely a complaint, had been transformed by the news that they were going to have to sell their house and find somewhere cheaper. The discovery that a promised cruise to the Caribbean had been shelved was a secondary

27

blow that seemed to have altered her personality.

Eating a sandwich lunch in the kitchen, Clive could find no words of consolation to break the silence. He stared at the fridge door, to which a magnetized donkey had pinned the memo: CHEMISTRY DETENTION MONDAY. His daughter Charlotte had been no less scornful than her mother once she learned that the prospect of a laptop computer had receded into a misty and uncertain future.

But his relationship with his daughter had been difficult even before his journey into unemployment. Something happened to girls, he discovered, with the onset of puberty. Dad went from hero to zero, from god to sod, overnight. Her impatience with him was a mystery, and although he had been assured that a new rebellious, independent streak was not uncommon at that age, he found it painful. At ten, Charlotte had been a sheer delight.

What had hurt him most had been the discovery that she told her friends at school that she was an orphan. 'You don't think those people who pick me up from school are my parents, do you?' she had said to one of the girls in her class. Holly found this amusing, but Clive had felt shut out.

'I suppose we'll soon be hiding from the milkman,' Holly said in the kitchen. She had finished her sandwich and was drinking a glass of milk.

Clive, immersed in dark thoughts about his wayward daughter, looked at her in search of a meaning. 'Hiding from the milkman?'

'Unpaid bills. There's one here now for forty-five pounds.'

'We can pay it,' he told her. 'However, there are going to be other bills that will be difficult until we move.'

Holly finished her milk and put the empty glass down on the table with a little bang. 'Alternatively, you could get another job.'

Clive had spent the morning combing through the situations vacant columns in three newspapers. 'I think we've got to accept that a job at my age is going to be harder to find than a condom machine in the Vatican,' he said.

'What age is that, darling? There's your chronological age, your biological age and your psychological age. In your case, forty, thirty and twenty.'

Clive thought about this. He decided that she meant he was wearing well but had the mind of a child.

'Thanks,' he said.

'The trouble with you is the top six inches,'

she said, tapping her head. She gave him one of her meaningful looks that meant nothing to him. 'You seem to have lost your confidence along with your job.'

'Confidence is the feeling you have before you know better,' he told her.

'Why don't you talk to Brad? He's a man who knows how to shake the money tree. Or perhaps I should get a job?'

This was not a possibility that had occurred to Clive. There was some residual secretarial know-how from an earlier incarnation, but the new technology had rendered it as redundant as a talent for darning socks.

'I hope that won't be necessary,' he said, standing up. He left the kitchen, not liking its heat, and crept away to the sitting room where he sank depressed, into an armchair. Perhaps television could provide an escape from the present horror. The previous night, for the first time, he had had a dream about Holly that was not wholly flattering. She had been kidnapped, and he received a ransom note in which all the letters had been cut from newspaper headlines. It said: WE HAVE YOUR WIFE. IF WE DON'T RECEIVE £5,000 BY SUNDAY WE'RE GOING TO BRING HER BACK.

He picked up one of her magazines that lay on the arm of the chair. A scarlet headline on the cover said: 'I had my throat stapled and lost 18 stone!' He put it down, feeling queasy, and found a newspaper instead. In Rome a man had been cleared of rape because the woman was wearing jeans. Judges decided that it wasn't possible to remove them without the woman's consent.

Clive was considering the flaws in this judicial opinion when the phone rang. Holly answered it in the hall and he waited to hear what intrusion from the outside world had breached their defences. When Holly appeared at the door, she was displaying considerably less aplomb than had been on show in the kitchen.

'It's Charlotte,' she said flatly. 'They found her drunk.'

'Drunk?'

'Lying on the ground drunk. She's in the school sick quarters. We've got to go to fetch her.'

Clive shot out of his chair. He was becoming accustomed to disasters of one sort and another, but this one took him by surprise. When Holly left the room to change for the journey, he just stood there, stunned, trying to imagine how his fifteen-old daughter could get drunk at school. He pulled himself together and went out to get the BMW from the garage.

For a while they travelled in silence, each absorbing their news. Then Holly said: 'Do you think she was drinking because you lost your job? Do you think she was worried about losing the house?'

He could see — he should have known — that he was somehow going to get the blame for this, and he brushed the idea aside irritably. 'She was experimenting with alcohol, Holly. She wasn't drowning her sorrows.'

'Experimenting? She was mullered.'

It irked him even more that his wife was now using the vocabulary of their daughter. The lexicon of the playground had required his constant attention. Fit meant attractive and minging and munting meant bad. Fat meant cool and yuk meant no food, thanks. He struggled to keep up.

'I'm not convinced that school is the right place for children today,' he said. 'It's where all the bad influences are. And they don't seem to have ordinary lessons like English and algebra. It's food technology, design and instrumental enrichment.' He had tried to discuss this with Charlotte recently, and she had informed him solicitously that if brains were dynamite he wouldn't have enough to blow the wax out of his ears — another verbal souvenir from the playground.

They found her lying on the floor with her

face in a white plastic bowl. A young teacher was sitting on a chair nearby, watching this unlovely scene with perceptible disinterest. She stood up when they came in.

'She's being sick,' she said unnecessarily. 'I have to stay with her in case she chokes on her vomit.'

'Do you know what happened?' Clive asked.

'It looks as if her friend stole a bottle of sherry from somewhere and they drank the lot in the lunch hour.'

'What happened to the other girl?' Holly asked.

'I think Charlotte drank most of it.'

Charlotte, a pretty blonde just like her mother, turned her head on hearing their voices.

'I'm sorry, Mummy. I'm sorry, Daddy,' she said indistinctly. It was a long time since she had apologized for anything, and Clive realized how drunk she must be. The world was moving too quickly for him, he decided. He had enjoyed his first beer at a party at seventeen, and now, at fifteen, his daughter was more drunk than he had ever been.

The sick quarters consisted of one single bed and a sink, but Charlotte, in her present state, had not been entrusted with either. The teacher, a girl in her late twenties with big, round spectacles and a pale, flat face, looked as fed up as he was. Clive wondered what factors had nudged her into teaching, which he thought a demanding and underpaid method of passing the time. She looked solemn and humourless, and if she was dealing with a hundred Charlottes every day he could see why. Life must be an unrewarding struggle to persuade teenagers that work was worthwhile in the long run, or to convince them that their future was being cast in stone while their attention was elsewhere.

The teacher bent over the prostrate centre of attention and asked briskly: 'Do you want to go home, Charlotte?'

An ambiguous groan from the floor left this question open, and so Clive and Holly, evidently detained here indefinitely, sat on the bed which was covered with an old grey blanket.

'What did the headmaster say?' Clive asked.

'He's away at a conference today, but I expect he'll want to talk to you.'

'I think I'll want to talk to him,' Clive said. 'I never saw any alcohol in the years that I was school. What happened to *in loco parentis*?'

The teacher's face stiffened, and she

looked as if she had something to say about this, but then decided that it wasn't her place to do so.

Outside a change-of-class bell rang in the hall.

'How are you feeling now, dear?' Holly asked her daughter. Holly's principal emotion here seemed to be embarrassment at the situation she was in. The anger would probably come later.

After a while it was clear that Charlotte had stopped being sick, but was in danger of falling asleep on the floor. Clive moved across to her and bent down.

'Come on, kid. We're going home.'

When she opened her eyes they seemed unfocused. The profile presented to him was devoid of colour.

'OK,' she whispered.

He lifted her to her feet and supported her as they walked out to the car. Clive felt vaguely cheated. Now that he could justifiably have a go at her there was no point to it. She had suffered enough already, and would feel even worse tomorrow.

4

The estate agent's sign that was erected outside the Devlins' home with 'For Sale' in large blue letters was like an admission of defeat. It represented an announcement to the neighbours that the Devlin family had failed in some crucial area of their lives, and its prominent position made it a constant and unwelcome reminder that those lives were about to change.

It was a source of mild surprise to Andy that his phlegmatic wife took to the impending upheaval with something approaching enthusiasm, and seemed to spot an opportunity where he saw only failure. Perhaps she had secretly hated the house or, possibly, the neighbours.

She developed a theory once the house was on the market that the visitors' nostrils should be assailed by a pleasant aroma as they stepped into the hall. She said that coffee was acceptable, but the chances of a sale would be greatly enhanced if they were baking bread.

Andy declined to retrain as a baker and learned to hate the time-wasting intruders with their suspicious glances and imbecilic questions. 'Where will I put my boat?' one putative purchaser asked. Andy glowered at him but didn't reply. The cheery demeanour of the salesman wasn't easily fabricated.

Meanwhile, the windows were spotless and the brass glinted. Extraneous possessions were stowed away and the vacuum cleaner was perpetually warm.

Four couples had already been ushered through their crowded home. One loved the house but thought the garden was too small. Another liked the garden but found the lay-out of the house wasn't to their taste. A third couple gave the impression that they were on a grand tour — that this was one of a dozen houses they were looking at today and by tonight they wouldn't remember which was which. Looking at houses was a national hobby: there was no law which said you had to buy one.

Two weeks into this painful exercise, Andy lay face down on his bed in the prostrate position of a vanquished fighter. Submission, capitulation, surrender seemed appropriate reactions to the rebuffs and reverses which plagued his life. Energy came from optimism, but the wells of optimism had run dry. Downstairs, with quiet energy, Clare was making herself a skirt, reconciled to the melancholy fact that no money would arrive to buy a new one. Andy had watched this endeavour with feelings of shame, and, on the bed, sought to push his thoughts towards more profitable pastures.

Sir Walter Raleigh, locked up in the Tower for thirteen endless years on the flimsiest of evidence, didn't lie defeated on his bed. He wrote the first volume of his *History of the World*, and planned a gold-seeking expedition to the Orinoco. Let Sir Walter be an example to the downtrodden and demoralized, Andy told himself.

The doorbell rang; he rolled off the bed and stood up. Perhaps it was the bailiff with distrainment in mind. It was difficult to see what he could take unless he was going to stagger off with the fridge on his back. But perhaps other things in the house, previously regarded as worthless, were now beginning to attain an antique value: his typewriter looked like a museum piece, the television no longer resembled those you saw in shop windows, and the bathroom scales had never heard of kilograms. Step forward into the past.

But the couple Clare was admitting to the hall when he peered apprehensively down the stairs were after more than the fridge. They wanted, or thought they wanted, the house. He went down to meet them.

They were a young couple named Havers, probably not yet thirty, and they evinced more than the customary scepticism when offered information. Like an aggressive political interviewer, they expected to hear lies. Occasionally they prodded a wall with a finger as if the house had been constructed on the San Andreas fault and would need special resilience.

At the window, Mr Havers looked up at the uncertain autumn sky and asked 'Where's the sun?'

'It rises over there,' Andy told him, 'and shines on the patio in the afternoon and evening.'

'It's perfect,' Clare assured him.

Havers' response to this was to produce a compass from his pocket with which he checked exactly where the sunset would fall. 'You're right,' he said, but Andy couldn't muster a civil reply. When Clare took the visitors upstairs for a meticulous examination of three bedrooms and a small bathroom, Andy fetched his coat, made an excuse and left.

He had to collect his son from school. It was a job that he enjoyed — it got him away from the desk — but his arrival at the school gates embarrassed Greg. All the other parents collecting their beloved offspring were women, and Greg was asked why his father didn't have a job. He was at an age when children didn't like to be different.

Andy got into the Golf and checked the petrol: running out was a constant possibility in his financial situation, and to do so when Greg was in the car would invite ridicule of the most hurtful kind.

His relationship with his son was one that he conducted warily. He knew that everything was remembered and would come back to him when Greg was twenty or thirty. The news that they had to sell the house had been accepted silently but Andy, susceptible now to paranoia along with many another mental affliction, thought he detected a cooling in what had once been a wonderful friendship.

Greg came out of the school, cap askew, a collection of books tucked under one arm, and got into the front seat of the Golf without speaking.

'A good day?' Andy asked, starting the engine.

'OK,' said Greg, placing the books carefully on the floor between his feet. 'Weldon's a geek.'

Andy, trying to remember who Weldon was, glanced at his son. He was a small, muscular little boy with bright eyes and his mother's black hair. Its cut at the moment was the ugliest that Andy had seen — the bottom half shaved and the top trimmed in a straight line round his head.

'Why's that?' he asked.

'I thought he was talking about David Beckham, but he was talking about some writer. He knew I wasn't listening and asked me what I could tell him about Beckett. I said he married Posh Spice and the class went crazy. Got anything to eat?'

'Wait till dinner. You'll spoil your appetite.'

In a mini-outburst of fury, the reply came back: 'God, dad, you're a bore.'

Andy drove carefully down a tree-lined avenue where children released from school were quite capable of rushing out in front of his wheels. He was trying to remember what he had been like at ten and suspected that the answer was more reverential. The pressures on children today were not good, it seemed to him. A frankness about sex and drugs, explicit newspapers, four-letter words tossed from the television. A different type of child, more knowing but less loveable, was being created.

'What else did you do today?' he asked. 'Apart from marry off a Nobel prize-winner to a Spice Girl?'

Greg stared at the street scene in front of him as he struggled to recall the tedium of his day. 'Mr Randall talked about God. The Muslims in our class were well impressed. What do you believe, Dad? Did God create the world?'

Andy was slightly taken aback by the directness of the question: it was some time since his son had consulted him about anything. But where religion was concerned he had some definite views. All over the world, as he saw it, children were brainwashed on the subject as soon as they got out of their prams. Their heads were filled with pernicious rubbish before they had reached their teens, and soon afterwards, convinced by moronic parents that their views were the right views and must prevail, they were throwing bottles or bombs. It happened from Belfast to Beirut. If Andy ever discussed religion or politics with his son, he never released the slightest hint about what he believed himself.

'Some people think so,' he murmured.

'But if God created the world, why did he wait 400 million years before putting people in it?' Greg asked.

Another reason for not preaching to your son was that he would hit you with a question that you didn't expect and couldn't answer just when you thought you had wrapped the subject up.

'Prolonged coffee break, perhaps?' he suggested.

Greg was considering this as they swung into the drive. Clare was waiting for them at the door.

'The estate agent has just phoned up,' she said. 'The Havers want to buy at the full asking price.'

'I was afraid they would,' said Andy gloomily.

5

It was with only the faintest tremor of apprehension that Brad Rowe fingered the insurance company's cheque for £30,000. In his line of business too many other cheques that not everybody would describe as having been earned had winged their way into his bank account. But he was surprised at how easy it had been.

'I can't imagine how they stole it,' he told the insurers disconsolately. 'I've still got the ignition key in my pocket.'

It was Olivia, rising drowsily from a nine-hour pill-induced slumber, who had discovered the empty garage. She had rushed to Brad's bedside, surprised that he was still asleep. She put it down to the strain of yesterday, not knowing that he had only been in bed for three hours.

'Brad!' she said, shaking him. 'The Bentley's gone!'

'Gone where?' he asked, still half asleep.

'How do I know? It's been stolen, you pillock.'

He was awake now, and knew that some acting was needed. 'Oh no,' he moaned. 'Not my Bentley!' The feigned misery tugged at his wife's heartstrings.

'Don't they think we have suffered enough?' she cried, without revealing who these malevolent but anonymous persecuters were. Brad phoned the police in his dressing gown and was able to show real anger at their apparent disinterest. But he knew that the call would be logged and would be an important fact when he contacted the luckless insurance company who would want to know whether the police had been notified and what the crime's number was. In the end he was driven to the conclusion that car thefts were now so prevalent that insurers hardly had time to write out the cheques without spending hundreds of hours investigating the circumstances of each disappearance.

Olivia's enthusiasm for the Bentley had been surprisingly short-lived. Her restless interest moved on effortlessly to more luxurious motors and it was obvious today that she preferred the cheque in the hand to the vehicle that was no longer in the garage.

'A tax-free thirty grand!' she said, closing her eyes to better imagine the things this would buy.

Brad, aware that unspent money made his wife uneasy, told her: 'It's going to pay the mortgage. It's going to save the house.'

'Not all of it,' Olivia said firmly. 'There's an outfit in Sloane Street I've got my eye on.'

They sat in the conservatory with their morning coffee. Brad, trying to adjust to leisure that he had never had, daydreamed of a comeback, a resurrection, a return to power, security and prosperity.

'I keep thinking the agency's still there,' he said sadly. 'It's like having a foot amputated, and it still itches.'

The metaphysical abstraction deflected his wife from her surreal shopping spree. 'I wonder whether a eunuch scratches his balls?' she asked.

Brad gave her a look which would have chilled a more vulnerable woman, but said nothing. He had never been very successful at penetrating her mind, and had never relied on her help in accumulating money. Her role was at the dispersal end. She took vitamin pills and blue algae juice every morning, attended yoga three times a week and had now taken up acupuncture to give her energy and boost the immune system. What Brad wanted more than anything else was a drink.

He borrowed Olivia's Audi and took the cheque to the bank. He could imagine the standing orders that were queueing up to devour it, and the thought propelled him involuntarily into an adjacent wine bar.

'There's nothing like a bottle of red wine to convince a man that life is worth living,' he told the barman.

The barman produced a new bottle, pulled the cork and poured a glass. But when he went to remove the bottle, Brad leaned over the counter and grabbed him by the wrist.

'Leave the bottle,' he said.

The man pulled his wrist free. 'We serve it by the glass,' he said.

Brad looked at him. He was surprised at how easily he could become angry since the firm collapsed, but there was no backing down now. 'I said leave the bottle. You can count the glasses.'

The man, unsure what to do, put the bottle down and then stood there staring at Brad. Brad was too busy drinking the wine to notice this glare but eventually became aware of it.

'I can see you've got something on what we might as well refer to as your mind,' he said.

'We can ban anyone we like, you know,' the barman told him.

'Really?' said Brad. 'What do you do with people you don't like?'

The barman moved away and resumed his glaring from a distance. Brad refilled his glass. He was quite happy to drink on his own, but this pleasure was to be denied him. A youngish man came in and sauntered up to

47

the counter. He wore shabby jeans and a yellow T-shirt which bore the message IF I HAD A LITTLE HUMILITY I'D BE PERFECT. He had long blond hair in a ponytail and was deeply tanned. After his white wine arrived he looked at Brad, wanting a conversation, but Brad ignored him. When you were out of work and went for a drink, he thought, these were presumably the sort of people you drank with. He felt as if he had made a sideways shift into another world. When he refilled his glass the barman called across to him: 'That's three.'

'Keep counting,' said Brad.

The ponytailed man, sensing disharmony, declared: 'Everybody should go to Bombay for a week. They'd be nicer to people.'

Peacemaker in a ponytail, Brad thought. He hated ponytails: he could never forget what was under a pony's tail. He drank his wine and hoped to be left alone, but it was apparent that the man was several drinks ahead of him.

'All the world's a stage, and all the men and women merely players,' he said now, as if illuminating a great truth that had escaped lesser minds.

'If all the world's a stage, where are the audience sitting?' Brad found himself replying. The wine was loosening his tongue, too.

48

The ponytailed man looked at him. 'Who was that poet whose face needed ironing?'

'Auden?'

'That's him. He had a nice line about taking your proper share of drink and dope. He knew, you see.'

He now lit with a very old Zippo lighter what might have been a cigarette, although Brad was beginning to wonder whether he was stoned.

'It was an addiction to cigarettes that killed my father,' he said conversationally.

'Really?'

'Crossed the road to buy a packet and got hit by a bus.' He gave Brad a wink. 'You got a wife?'

Brad wondered whether to answer this. He had come in here to escape, not to get button-holed by a man who, aside from a certain individuality, betrayed the odd hint of the authentically loopy.

'I believe I have,' he said.

'Smart, is she?'

'Pretty smart.'

'Give me a moronic tart with big knockers every time. Marriage? Half the pleasure for twice the price.'

The man, who Brad thought would surely repel all but the most desperate of women, talked as if he had prepared his script before

49

he came in. Perhaps he was an out-of-work actor.

'What makes you drink in wine bars,' he asked him, 'rather than pubs?'

'I like wine,' the man answered. 'Also, I've been banned from my favourite pub.'

'How sad. What happened?'

'A harmless little joke, but people don't have the sense of humour these days, I find.'

'And the joke was?'

'I taught the pub parrot to shout 'Wanker!' It took me two hours and lost the place five customers. One of them said, 'I didn't come in here to be insulted, at least not by a parrot'.'

The bar was clearly going to remain fairly empty until the lunchtime workers arrived breathlessly to discuss their love lives or office grievances, and the two men sat under the vigilant and hostile gaze of the barman, who had taken to recording Brad's glasses of wine on a large sheet of pink paper. The red walls of the bar were broken up by plants and posters. The plants, cheap artificial greenery, trailed from brown pots between large colourful pictures of favourite foreign tourist spots — Venice, Barcelona, Paris, Copenhagen — designed to lift the hearts of the assembled tipplers. It wasn't a large bar, but from beyond a fake wall behind the counter came the sounds of crockery and cooking pans as more staff prepared lunches. Obsessed by the fate of his own firm, Brad began to wonder how a business like this made money. The premises, the rent, the lighting and heating, the cooking facilities, the wages, the local taxes, the insurance, the accountants, the legal advice. Where was the revenue to match bills like that?

The question brought back dispiriting memories from his immediate past and he decided that he would only shake them off by leaving. He was beaten to it by his new friend, who was slapping his pockets and finding them empty.

'I'm going,' he said. 'To hell in a handcart, actually.'

'Why not?'

'Quite. The fires of hell hold few terrors if you plan to be cremated.'

He marched out of the door and Brad stood up and found some money. The barman came over, relieved to see it.

'Do you know who that was?' he asked.

Brad shook his head.

'Jason Marr.'

'Never heard of him.'

He escaped to the street and reached in his pocket for his mobile phone, but in his new laidback, jobless world he hadn't bothered to bring it. Driving home at midday after drinking a bottle of red wine was the sort of thing he carefully avoided: he valued his driving licence too highly. He found a phone kiosk and rang Olivia.

'I think you'd better pick me up,' he told her.

'Pick you up?' his wife replied irritably. 'How can I? You've got my car, you pillock.'

6

It occurred to Clive Preston, in the dark days which followed, that the second casualty of his uninhibited performance on the office desk was going to be his marriage. There was something about Holly's attitude towards him which suggested that she didn't like him very much and had only put up with him in the past because he was an established and reliable source of money. Clive, who could have understood this behaviour if Holly had known the truth about his sacking, began to wonder how they had married in the first place. What did they have in common? He made a list.

CLIVE	HOLLY
Red wine	White wine
White coffee	Black coffee
Steak	Fish
BBC	ITV
Broadsheet	Tabloid
Left wing	Right wing
Sun	Snow

Cats	Dogs
Bath	Shower
Planes	Ships
Marks & Spencer	Harrods
Beer	Champagne
Cornwall	Brighton
Spain	Switzerland

What they did have in common was Charlotte.

The teenage tyrant, recovered from her binge, had developed fanciful dreams about her future. The blind faith of youthful aspiration, untouched by life's disappointments, led her to believe that a career as an actress awaited her — not the theatre or the cinema, but the one-eyed monster in the corner that everybody watched. Charlotte's generation had latched on to a modern rule: if you didn't appear on television you didn't exist, and obscurity was for muppets.

She was approaching sixteen, a milestone which suggested liberation. She could buy cigarettes, do the Lottery, get married. It was time to arrange her future.

While Clive applauded her ambition, he could see no sign that she understood work would be needed to achieve it. Her approach to the coming O-level exams was cursory and the teachers' predictions depressing. He wondered whether she was still drinking.

The visit to the headmaster had been a chastening experience. Mr Speed, a man approaching sixty, managed to make both Clive and Holly feel hopelessly out of date.

'Alcohol seems to be a problem here,' Clive had suggested.

'I've been head at four schools, Mr Preston, and alcohol was a problem at every one of them,' said Mr Speed. 'We stamp on it when we see it, but how much do we miss? The problem is its availability. When I was young you could only get drink in an off licence and they asked your age. Now there's aisles of the stuff in supermarkets and anyone can buy it. There's always a helpful customer who will take it through the check-out for a polite youngster.'

'That's it, then?' said Holly, looking appalled. 'We resign ourselves to fifteen-year-old drunks?'

'Certainly not,' said Mr Speed soothingly. He had a small grey moustache which somehow suggested a sternness that evidently wasn't there. 'We fight it when we find it, but quite frankly alcohol isn't the main problem. Drugs are cheaper over a long night and more effective. They're a rite of passage now. Do you know that more than a quarter of a million young people take Ecstasy, cocaine or heroin every month?'

Clive left this depressing encounter feeling estranged from both Charlotte and Mr Speed. The world had changed when he wasn't looking, and he wasn't sure he could catch up.

'How did you get on with Speedy Gonzalez?' Charlotte asked that evening.

'He said that you were a very naughty girl,' Clive told her.

A mask of resentment, a recent addition to the changing appearances brought about by hair styling, eye shadow and no doubt other aids that Clive didn't like to investigate, had now taken up permanent residence on her face.

'Well, pants to him. He's rank. He has a few Britney Spears himself, I've heard.'

They were eating a cheap dinner of chicken and rice while the shrill abuse essential to a soap opera drifted across to them from a portable television in the corner.

'Britney Spears?' asked Clive.

'Beers. You don't want to know what a Brad Pitt is.'

She was right. He didn't. He asked: 'You think you could handle it in one of these soaps? Can you talk the language?'

'Wossup?'

'By George, she's got it,' said Holly.

'All I need is to get into acting school. Which is the best?'

'RADA is thought to be rather good.'

'They'll adore me.'

★ ★ ★

A few evenings later, Andy rang up and demanded that Clive come out for a drink.

'Of course, you may have to pay for them,' he said, 'but it's my last night here. We're moving tomorrow and then we'll be light years away.' In fact he was moving twenty miles, but if you drank a lot when you met a twenty-mile drive was a risky undertaking for people who depended on their cars.

Clive's house sale was lagging some way behind Andy's. It wasn't impelled by the same financial disasters. But there was a buyer now, moving dates were being discussed, and feeling every bit as displaced as his friend he went off to meet him.

They used a pub called the Hen and Chicken, a small friendly place that was within walking distance and had been untouched by modern innovations. The landlord, a jovial, red-faced ex-naval man called Eddie, was distressed to hear that he was about to lose two customers. He was sharing this grief with Brad when Clive arrived.

'You're only losing customers,' Brad told him. 'I'm losing friends.' He stood at the bar with his pint and his panatella, looking like a man who had lost the will to live. 'I'm a very emotional person,' he said. 'I can cry at the weather forecast.'

'Well, don't cry in here,' said Andy. 'Watering the beer is Eddie's job.'

'You could always come round and pick us up in the Bentley,' said Clive. 'I love luxurious cars.'

'Didn't you hear? It's been nicked.'

When Brad told the story of his vanished car, a story that began with Olivia dragging him from a deep sleep, he believed every word of it. His long, cold night in Dorset seemed to have dissolved in the memory bank.

'You poor sod,' said Andy. 'It's one thing after another.'

Brad shook his head in shared incomprehension at life's iniquities. He was an adroit and tireless liar — it was his stock-in-trade in the fashionable offices where he had recently practised his craft. Andy and Clive were, he knew, honest men, and gullibility was the

58

weakness of the honest man. A liar never believed anybody.

'I'm really sorry, Brad,' said Clive. 'I suppose you'll get some insurance?'

Brad shrugged. 'I'm trying, but you know how those rats wriggle, particularly when there's nothing there for them to inspect.' Gratified by the sympathetic reaction to his story, he bought a round of drinks with the insurance money, foaming pints of a locally produced bitter which was currently much in favour. 'What about you, Clive?' he asked. 'How are things with you?'

'My fifteen-year-old daughter has taken up getting drunk, and my wife seems to have decided that all men are feckless bozos. Apart from that, life's a carnival.'

'Mr Devlin? The usual litany of grievances, I suppose?'

'There'll be a marginal improvement tomorrow when we move. I'll get a cheque on the house sale.'

'You ought to be getting some unemployment money,' Brad told him. 'The golden rule is that if you don't sponge off the state, the state will sponge off you.'

'The trouble is that I am never quite sure that I am unemployed. I'm writing a play at the moment. It's a full-time job. The fact that I'll probably never earn a penny from it doesn't concern the Social Security people. They'd call me a self-employed writer, not unemployed.'

'You seem to have discovered a little poverty trap of your own and fallen into it,' Clive said admiringly. 'What's the play about?'

Andy sipped his beer thoughtfully. He was reluctant to talk about what he was writing. In its early stages the edifice was too fragile to withstand criticism, and a harsh remark could cause him to revise the whole idea or even abort the project. The impetus to keep writing, he found, needed constant protection.

But, encouraged by the drink, he embarked on the story of Walter Raleigh's remarkable life, and how it might be broken down into three coherent acts. Fortunately, he hadn't got very far when he saw that he had lost the attention of Clive, who was now focusing on some unseen development over Andy's shoulder. The view thus afforded him did strange things to his face. Vertical lines appeared on his forehead as his eyebrows moved towards each other. His bottom lip dropped, as if deserting the rest of his mouth.

'My God,' he said. 'It's Sandra.'

'Sandra?' said Brad. 'Who's she?'

Clive had abandoned the facial distortions

and developed a new posture which required him to bend his lanky frame forward on the stool so that his face was only inches from his knees. This exercise effectively removed him from Sandra's line of vision.

'Sandra is the cleaning lady,' he muttered.

Andy's head shot round instinctively. He saw a rather attractive woman with long blonde hair in her early thirties. She was wearing a brown check trouser suit and buying herself a gin and tonic a few yards down the bar.

'She doesn't look like a cleaning lady to me,' observed Brad. 'Tasty, I'd call her.'

'Yeah, well, they're not all old trouts with wrinkled stockings and moustaches,' said Clive. 'What's she doing in here?'

'The fact that not all her lovers have been stuffed to the gills with Viagra could have something to with it,' Andy suggested. 'You've got a fan.'

'She's had the hors-d'oeuvre. She's come back for the main course,' explained Brad.

'Hors-d'oeuvre?' said Clive. 'It was twenty-four hours before I could walk properly.'

'You're a star,' said Andy. 'Sit up and accept your new obligations.'

Clive cowered. Not much had gone right lately but he thought that at least this wretched incident had been consigned to the past. How on earth had the woman found him? He summoned up the courage to peer over Andy's shoulder and found that she was looking straight at him. A warm smile transformed her face and she was on the move.

'You look like a rabbit that's spotted a stoat,' said Brad, but she had reached them now.

'Mr Preston!' she said with a mixture of pleasure and surprise. 'Fancy seeing you!' She had a classless cockney voice of the type that you heard a lot on television.

'Sandra!' said Clive, who did indeed look more like the prey than the predator. 'What brings you to these parts?'

She was wondering whether a quick jump was out of the question, Andy wanted to say, but he kept his mouth shut and watched the embarrassed Clive with silent amusement.

'My sister lives over there,' Sandra said, waving an arm vaguely. Close up, she looked rather tired, but you could see that she must have been a pretty teenager. Her purifying perambulations through the grey-blue sky-scraper beside the Thames, where Clive had once deployed a cleansing and curing army of his own, stirred the blood of those younger members of the staff who were still untrammelled by domestic responsibilities.

Sexy Sandra, she was called. Clive, aware of her renown, had kept well clear until the Viagra unglued him.

'How's the office?' he asked, finding nothing to say.

'Missing you,' said Sandra with a playful smile. 'Still, you left them something to think about.'

'I hope they've stopped thinking about it,' Clive replied despondently.

'*They* may have,' said Sandra, and her meaning was clear. 'So you live round here?'

'With my wife and daughter,' he said, parading his family like a talisman that would protect him from evil influences.

'Nice,' said Sandra. 'I've got a daughter as well.'

'How old?'

'Fifteen.'

'What?' said Andy. 'You're not old enough to have a daughter of fifteen.'

Her girlish hairstyle, pert nose, sexy eyes and rosy cheeks, along with a firm, shapely body that the check trouser suit did nothing to conceal, did suggest something younger than the mother of a teenager. Clive was confused, but in Andy and Brad she had found an enthusiastic audience.

'Well,' she said, 'I was seventeen when I had her.'

'I'm Andy, by the way,' said Andy, 'and this is Brad. I'm afraid Mr Preston's social graces vanished with his job.'

'You should have seen him when he was a galloping centre-half,' said Brad. 'Patrolling the midfield like a demented giraffe.'

'He's a man of great energy,' said Sandra.

Clive saw which way the conversation was going, and swiftly deflected it.

'Does your daughter drink?' he asked.

'Drink?'

'My daughter is also fifteen and she got drunk the other day.'

'That's terrible,' said Sandra, shaking her head in disbelief. 'I don't think my daughter drinks. I don't see her as much as I'd like to. She's at a rather good boarding school in Kent.'

Clive was rapidly becoming inured to shocks and surprises, but he was still taken aback by this. His own daughter, in keeping with his trenchant left-wing beliefs, was being educated at a state comprehensive while the cleaning lady's was being polished and refined at a posh boarding school in the country. His mind spun. What differences would you see when they were both twenty? What differences would you see now?

'That must cost a bit,' Andy suggested.

'She got a scholarship which cut the fees,'

Sandra told him. 'My father and sister help a bit, and I've got two jobs.'

'Two more than me,' said Clive. 'At forty I've got a great future behind me.'

Feeling himself marooned here, the idiot sinner among a trio of failures, he saw his fall from grace and his reaction to it as even more ignominious whcn he contrasted it with Sandra's cheerful acceptance of a humble life packed with work. When she left reluctantly, for a dinner date with her sister, the three men were all left with the disturbing impression that she was handling her life better than any of them.

'A great girl,' said Brad. 'I bet you meet her again. I've seen that look in a woman's eyes before. Next thing you know your trousers are missing.'

But Clive, alarmed at this possibility, found a glimmer of hope.

'I'm moving,' he said tersely. 'She won't know where I am.'

7

Andy Devlin sat at his desk in the smallest bedroom of his new rented home and tried to work. There was some money now from the house sale, but after the debts had been settled it wasn't going to last very long, and his status had changed. If you failed to pay the mortgage you got a discreet approach from the building society; if you didn't pay the rent you were thrown into the street. He needed to earn.

His desk was covered with notes, all connected with what was now his main project. He read and reread them.

Walter Raleigh, the boy from Hayes Barton, Devon, was knighted at the early age of thirty-two. He was a great favourite at the court of Queen Elizabeth, a soldier, explorer, historian and poet who had sent three expeditions to America and been responsible for the introduction of potatoes and tobacco to England. But when he seduced Bessy Throckmorton, one of the Queen's maids of honour, Her Majesty was upset, having fancied him herself. She sent him to the Tower. On his release he married Bessy and left London for Sherborne. When Elizabeth died, Raleigh's enemies turned James I against him and he was thrown back in the Tower on a trumped-up charge of treason. A death sentence was commuted to life imprisonment. After thirteen years he was released on the promise that he would lead an expedition to the Orinoco and find gold. The expedition was a failure. The earlier death sentence was invoked, and he was beheaded at sixty-six.

Considering this wealth of material, Andy wondered whether it should be a musical. The competition for the role of Bessy Throckmorton would be intense, and the songs would write themselves. 'Anyone For A Fag?' would be a certain smash, and an up-to-date version of 'Walter, Walter, Lead Me To The Altar!' would give Bessy her show-stopper.

As Shakespeare was a contemporary who was knocking around in the same circles at the time, Andy had a plan to introduce them. Who knew whether they ever met? Perhaps the poet Raleigh helped the poet Shakespeare with his plays. Perhaps he wrote a couple of them. As Shakespeare had shown, history was something a writer could tamper with.

The house which had suddenly become the Devlins' home provided a powerful incentive to work harder. Its tiny rooms and limited facilities made him yearn for a better place to live. There was no central heating, no downstairs lavatory, no utility room for washing machine and fridge. These last two were crammed into the kitchen, leaving room for only the smallest table. For heating they had to rely again on coal fires, and Andy found himself chopping logs for the first time in years.

Clare's reaction to these inconveniences was to get a job. She slipped out one morning and returned with a triumphant smile. She had been hired to help with the food preparation in a delicatessen, starting next week. The more they earned, she said, the greater their chances of moving to a better home.

Andy was astounded and impressed. He also felt guilty. The literary lottery was a nightmare, but he had no desire to be interviewed by people who would imprison him in their airless offices for insulting remuneration. It would seal his future. With an optimism that owed nothing to experience, he returned to Act Two.

Scene: The Tower
ELIZABETH
I thought better of you, Walter.

68

I am Miss Throckmorton's moral
guardian. Perhaps a taste of
celibacy will clear your head.
RALEIGH
I don't know what I can say,
Your Majesty.
ELIZABETH
Say nothing. Your deeds have
spoken louder than any words.

It was going well. Andy was in the Tower now
and could see Raleigh standing, his head
contritely bowed, before his irate sovereign.
The difficulty would be in conveying the
personal disappointment felt by the Queen at
Raleigh's sexual betrayal. An element of royal
jealousy was required. Her official disapproval
was easier to handle.

He was pondering this when Clare came in
with the post. He had never managed to
persuade her not to interrupt him when he
was writing, and given the meagre returns his
writing produced he had never felt strong
enough to labour the point.

The previous evening, to celebrate her new
job, she had opened a bottle of sparkling
wine. Her delight at finding work was in no
way dampened by the fact that they couldn't
lash out on champagne. Andy hugged her. He
loved her pretty face, her bright mind, her

69

extraordinary tolerance of the deprivations he was imposing on her with the precarious existence he blindly pursued. Her resilience in the face of succeeding disasters and her refusal to complain could bring him to the edge of tears. There was something saint-like about her and he wanted nothing more than to cover her with money.

'Why do you put up with it?' he asked her.

She gave him a kiss and clinked her glass against his. 'I've got faith in you,' she said.

'But this new house — it's awful. And we don't know where the next pound is coming from.'

She sat on the kitchen table and crossed her legs. Andy followed this movement: he loved her knees.

'It's true that most people's income gradually goes up, and yours gradually goes down,' she said. 'It makes you different from the others.'

'Different and worse.'

'Andy, if I'd wanted an accountant for a husband I'd have married one. There *were* offers.'

'I'm sure there were. You're a stunning lady and you deserve better than me.'

He felt genuine remorse at the impoverished situation he had placed her in, a remorse made worse by the fact that she never mentioned the things that were denied her — new clothes, cosmetics, kitchen aids, hairdressing appointments, theatre trips and holidays.

'Who knows who's better than you?' she said. 'You've hardly started yet.'

At that moment Greg, drained by the demands of his PlayStation, wandered in to join them. 'Daddy, will we always be poor?' he asked.

'Of course not, dear,' Clare assured him, while Andy coped with a fresh surge of guilt.

When she brought in the post the following morning, Clare also gave him a coffee. This was a luxury provided by the house sale money. For weeks he had been writing without the stimulation of caffeine.

'There's a card from Auntie Fay,' she said, handing him half a dozen envelopes. The post was no longer dominated by bills. They had been replaced by early Christmas cards. Andy had lost his train of thought now, and settled back to look at them. There was no chance that he would remember who Auntie Fay was — Clare's mother had seven sisters — but he worked his way through the cards, finding mostly brief messages from friends who only contacted him once a year.

But there was, he discovered, a depressing innovation in the Christmas card ritual. Some people were enclosing with their cards a photocopied bulletin of the year's family news, and these reports had an unwelcome triumphalist tone.

'It has been a wonderful year for the Bagnall family,' he read with a horror that grew. 'Things seem to get better and better! David was promoted again, so now we are hoping that he will be offered a seat on the board. How he found the time to redecorate the house, build a gazebo and win the men's singles at the tennis club I will never know!

'The children have been just as energetic. Tamsin, who celebrated her seventeenth birthday in the spring, got six straight As in her exams and is off to Cambridge after a year on a kibbutz. She finally finished the novel she has been working on for two years and now has her very own agent who is so impressed with her book that he has arranged an auction for publishers in New York.

'Oliver, at fourteen, is going through that uncertain stage which seems to afflict boys of that age, but he spends a lot of time with his guitar and has written several songs. It is something that he seems to be particularly good at, because two of them are going to be recorded by one of those groups with funny names like Desert or Oasis.'

The contrast this provided with his own life

was too much for Andy to bear. Incensed by the complacency, he pushed his play to one side and grabbed a new sheet of paper. Some more rewriting of history was required, and he was the man to do it.

'It's been a hell of a year for the Bagnall family,' he scribbled furiously. 'David is obviously going through some sort of midlife crisis, and spends most of his time with the witch next door who has responded to his puppy-like devotion by giving him a stupendous dose of clap. On Tuesday he came home with his bottom covered with lash marks, a mystery I haven't succeeded in unravelling. Naturally he was unsettled by the sudden redundancy notice, but you would have thought he could see that all his energies are now needed to get back into the jobs market. It's not something I can tell him because we no longer converse.

'I've got enough on my plate. Tamsin is six months pregnant and has been thrown out of school. I think the father is the Nigerian paperboy, but she is keeping her options open and won't discuss it until she sees what colour the baby is.

'Oliver's shoplifting spree ended in Boots where four overweight coppers pinned him to the floor and discovered that his pockets were stuffed with banana-flavoured condoms. His case comes up in the New Year when, by a cruel coincidence, we shall be in court ourselves for non-payment of council tax. To cap it all, the dog got run over.'

A bracingly revisionist piece of history, he decided, and returned, creatively satisfied, to his play which he hoped would embody these very qualities.

8

Brad Rowe discovered to his surprise that he no longer went out. Reclusive tendencies had taken over and his interest in the outside world waned. He could see that he was going to end up pottering around his garden, pruning, strimming, mulching and hoeing, but what was wrong with that? Fresh air and exercise was a preferable alternative to the stress-filled, alcohol-fuelled existence that had taken him, through years of hard work, from obscurity to total bloody oblivion. He had lost his job, his money, his car and his friends, and now, as time lay heavy on his hands, it was the friends he was missing most.

Clive had shuffled off, Oates-like, the previous week to a semi-detached house with his semi-detached wife and dissident daughter. The new home, in a cul-de-sac next to a cemetery fifteen miles away, was on the outskirts of a town that was completely devoid of character, a factor which kept the price of houses down in that area and made them attractive to the newly pauperized like Clive. Holly had escorted him to this new-found land with a face like ice.

Missing Clive and missing Andy, neither of whom had so far managed to establish a connection with the telephone company, Brad sat on a Saturday evening before a television set that was on but unwatched.

Olivia, in new four-inch Gucci suede mules which unknown to her had been procured by the revenue from a field in Dorset, had gone off in what was now the family's only car to slurp mint juleps or gin slings with the deluded bourgeoisie she regarded as her friends. Brad, not wanting to be quizzed on the downfall of Bradley Rowe Images by emaciated hostesses or toupeed tycoons, elected, as usual, to skip this soirée and stay at home.

The setbacks he had endured affected him more than he would have expected. He felt listless and had no energy. His brain ticked over but produced nothing helpful about his future. Going to bed was the high point of his day.

Feeling an ennui that could only be staved off by alcoholic anaesthetic, he went out to the kitchen and peeled a bottle of Veuve Clicquot. He would have a party on his own. How sad was that? He took the bottle and a glass back to the warmth of his lonely sofa.

The glowing rectangle burbled in front of him but he didn't have the concentration that it needed. The scene, as in most of the other programmes that he caught these days, was a hospital ward. It was not an attractive setting for a man who was already wrestling with hypochondria before incipient agoraphobia came beaming over the horizon. Since when had pain and sickness been regarded as entertainment?

Zombified by solitary drinking, he lacked the energy to reach for the remote, and sank instead into a hazy dreamworld where people ran along white beaches chasing colourful balloons that were always just out of their reach. Released from this teasing scene, he noticed that the programme had changed: doctors and nurses had been replaced by a row of smiling people who were being lobbed childishly simple questions with the bait of a world cruise for the winner being dangled before them. In some way that Brad couldn't quite work out, this little game was connected to the National Lottery which followed, but his attention drifted away again to faraway places where the sun shone and pressure was unknown. When he returned to the real world this time, numbered balls were swirling like snow in a drum.

Brad did not do the Lottery. He was not averse to the occasional gamble — on political developments rather than horses

— but he had read about odds of fourteen million to one on a Lottery ticket and not liked the chances. However, a few weeks ago after a wine bar session in which the Lottery had occupied much of the conversation, he had lurched, slightly buzzed, into an adjoining shop, filled in one line and paid for eight weeks. He hadn't looked at the ticket since and didn't even know where it was.

He sipped his champagne and stared bleary-eyed at the screen, where balls were now being dislodged from the drum. He imagined millions of people were gazing at this picture on their screens, believing that their problems were about to be solved. Optimism was the last refuge of the idiot, and reposing their hopes in a Lottery win showed how desperate people could become.

He made a successful grab for the remote to switch channels and escape from this nonsense when the four numbers already on the screen struck a chord in his mind: thirty-nine, thirty-eight, forty-one, forty. He couldn't remember the six numbers he had done but he remembered those. Having no better idea, he had done forty-one, forty and thirty-nine because they were his age, Clive's age and Andy's age. He had then added thirty-eight because it was Olivia's age. A friend who looked at his ticket afterwards said, 'Well, at least if you win you'll be the only winner.'

He pulled himself up on the sofa. He had been in danger of falling asleep, but he was focusing now. Four numbers sometimes paid £100 and in his present situation all contributions were gratefully received. All he had to do was find the ticket.

He got to his feet, pleased that he had something to do, and went upstairs to his office. It was a room that he had avoided since the firm's collapse: the memories that filled it were too painful. Files, folders and reference books were strewn over the desk where he had once sat in the evenings, catching up on work. Clipboards were propped against the wall, listing clients' demands and his staff's ideas for coping with them. Elaborate art work, suddenly no longer needed, lay neglected on the floor, and a chart on the wall vividly portrayed the gradual ascent and violent descent that was the story of Bradley Rowe Images.

It took an effort of will to rummage through these sad relics, and the Lottery ticket wasn't there. He left the office with relief and wondered if he would ever go in there again. Outside he stood still, trying to remember where he might have put a Lottery ticket. With his luck, he thought, it was probably safely buried in the dashboard pocket of the Bentley.

He moved to the bedroom and his voluminous wardrobe. Here a dozen suits, expensively collected from some of the best shops in Savile Row, were sharing his redundancy. In the one he had worn on the fateful last day he found a wallet. It was stuffed with credit cards and membership cards and, at the back, three £20 notes he didn't know he had. Pulling them out — happy to be reunited with them — he dislodged the Lottery ticket. He checked whether it was still valid, not quite remembering when he paid for eight weeks. It was. He carried it like a holy sacrament downstairs.

The Lottery programme had been replaced by some sort of chat show in which the host talked more than the guests, and Brad refilled his glass and switched to Ceefax. He always enjoyed flicking through the pages of Ceefax (See Facts) with its immediate news, city prices and sports results. Apart from anything else, it was quieter.

He punched five-five-five and six large yellow numbers appeared on the screen. He was relieved to see that his four were still there, that he hadn't made a silly mistake. The other numbers were thirty-five and forty-nine.

Gratified, he sat back on the sofa and took such a large swig of champagne that it became necessary to refill his glass. It was a long time since he had won anything or had something to celebrate. He turned off the television and took a slow sip from his newly filled glass. He wondered how Olivia was getting on among the successful people, as she delicately fended off questions about her husband's entrepreneurial triumphs. After half an hour of being grilled by that posturing mob it would probably dawn on her why he wasn't at her side.

He picked up the Lottery ticket again to enjoy his quadruple bull's-eye, and a strange feeling came over him. The other numbers, the two he hadn't bothered about, looked familiar. They were thirty-five and forty-nine. Hadn't he just seen them on the screen? He grabbed the remote, switched the set back on and then sat there tensely waiting for the Ceefax page to reappear. When it did, his heart took a lurch which he feared for a moment was terminal; his age and lifestyle placed him firmly in the heart-attack zone.

There on the screen were thirty-five and forty-one. He checked the numbers slowly, one by one, studying the screen and then his ticket. And then he knew that he had won and that his life was about to change for ever.

81

The discovery reduced him to gibbering idiocy. At first his bulky figure jumped round the room like a chained bear forced to entertain tourists, and then he was throwing his fist in the air and shouting 'Yeah!' like a simple-minded footballer. Breathlessness curtailed this flourish, and he slumped to the sofa, his heart pounding, and tried to figure out his next move. Firstly, he told himself, he should calm down.

Some action was obviously required of him, but he had to relax and think clearly. He picked up the Lottery ticket and looked at the back. How were you supposed to claim? The instructions in tiny pink type were impenetrable, but one line in bold type made sense to him: 'If you believe you have won a prize of more than £10,000 please phone the National Lottery Line.' He scanned the ticket for this number and eventually found it. A separate MINICOM line for the hard-of-hearing was also available.

How much did he believe he had won? Perhaps this was the day when thousands won and they got £9,000 each. He turned to the Ceefax page where the details would appear when Camelot's software had completed its bi-weekly miracle of assessing millions of tickets in less than an hour. He desperately wanted to tell somebody now, but his friends weren't on the phone, and so far as Olivia was concerned he wanted to see her face when the news hit her.

Within a few minutes the news hit him. Suddenly the screen was filled with information which he struggled to take in: the jackpot was £11.4 million, and there was only one winner. It had been a rollover, apparently, which accounted for the higher than usual jackpot. Four numbers were paying £92. The machine was Guinevere, and the set of balls number three . . .

This time the news numbed him. He sat on the sofa transfixed, but his head was spinning.

'Eleven point four million,' he said out loud, to make sure he was still functioning normally. 'Eleven point bloody four!' But he still sat there, trying to absorb the enormity of it, and it was ten minutes before he felt able to make a phone call.

The number on the ticket turned out to be a call centre in Aintree where a bored girl sounded as if she had already fielded a dozen calls from hoaxers, nutters, the hopelessly innumerate or just people who had mislaid their glasses. She asked him for the reference number on his ticket, where he had bought it, and his name, address and telephone number.

'I think I've won the big one,' he told her.

'You may have,' she said, not anxious to commit herself. 'None of the numbers are on the calendar, so all the people who do birthdays are out of it.'

'Do many people do birthdays?'

'Nearly all of them, apparently. Wait by your phone, Mr Rowe. We'll be calling you back very shortly.'

Ten minutes later Mr Chivers rang from the Lottery head office in Watford. Brad's status had undergone a drastic revision in this brief time, and Mr Chivers was appreciably warmer than the lonely telephone girl in Liverpool. He explained that every winner was allocated a winner's adviser and Brad had been granted the attention of Mr Chivers. In this role he was quite prepared to come round the following morning to provide emotional assistance or any other help that was required.

'I hope you don't think me unduly pushy,' Brad said, 'but when do I get the money?'

'On Monday,' said Mr Chivers.

'And where do I have to go?'

'Go? You don't go anywhere. We fetch you. I'll be at your front door with a car on Monday morning. Do you have a wife?'

'I do.'

'I'll be driving you both to London then. The champagne will be waiting.'

'Wonderful,' said Brad. 'Take Sunday off. I can handle the emotional turmoil. I've had a lot of practise.'

He replaced the phone and poured the remains of the champagne into his glass.

'Here's to me!' he said, raising the glass. 'A multi-millionaire at forty-one.'

The front door opened at that moment, and Olivia came in. She looked at him quizzically.

'Were you talking to yourself?' she asked.

'I was,' he agreed. 'I'm the only one who listens to me. Did you have a pleasant evening?'

She sat on the sofa and removed her new suede mules. They were probably better to look at than stand in for two hours.

'Very pleasant, thank you. They were disappointed not to see you.' She looked at the empty bottle. 'You've been drinking champagne on your own, have you?'

'I've been celebrating, darling. I've made some money.'

'You've made some money sitting on the sofa and getting drunk? That takes some believing.'

He wasn't sure he believed it himself now. The interruption of her arrival had stopped his triumphant train of thought, and the idea that he had won the Lottery now seemed a notion too improbable to sustain.

'It does seem odd, doesn't it? But it's been an odd sort of evening.'

'How much did you make, dear?' She was humouring him now.

'Just a few million,' he said. 'Nothing excessive.'

She gave him a hard, cool look, and then put one hand on her forehead. 'I'm afraid the collapse of the agency has left a mark on you, Brad. We'll soon be talking to the men in white coats.'

'Eleven point four million, actually,' he told her. 'It should challenge even your formidable spending powers.' He liked the sound of eleven point four. It must be worth thousands a day just in interest.

She looked at him again, taken by the preciseness of 'eleven point four'. 'What are you talking about, you pillock?'

He sat down beside her and put the ticket in her hand. While she looked at it he got up the Ceefax page.

'Compare the numbers, dear,' he said. 'In your own time. I know you're not a maths person.'

She stared at the screen and then at the ticket. 'Jesus,' she said, and started to cry. He put his arm round her. 'Eleven million?' she muttered into a dainty pink handkerchief.

'We'll be able to buy — '

'Anything,' said Brad.

'You clever bastard!'

'Half right,' said Brad. 'Do you want a coffee after all your socialite guzzling?'

'Please.'

When he brought it in she was still clutching the ticket, but had regained her poise. A more serious expression had replaced the tears.

'There won't be any publicity, will there?' she asked. 'I don't think I could bear the stigma of being a Lottery winner.'

★   ★   ★

Mr Chivers arrived at 9.30 on Monday morning in a pale blue Mercedes. He was younger than he had sounded on the phone, and seemed so happy that people might have mistaken him for the winner.

'Mr and Mrs Rowe,' he said, bowing graciously. 'Your carriage awaits.'

Brad and Olivia, who had been ready for an hour, got into the back seats of the car. Mr Chivers turned to them from the front.

'One thing I need to do, and would have done yesterday if I'd seen you, is check your ticket,' he said. He opened a brief-case and spent nearly a minute checking the precious piece of paper against documents he'd brought with him.

'Congratulations,' he said. 'Excuse me while I make a call.' Into his phone he said: 'I'm bringing Mr and Mrs Rowe to London. The ticket's fine. We'll be with you about eleven.'

'Where are we going?' Olivia asked when he finally started the engine. 'Cockspur Street. It's the London regional office.'

'Never heard of it,' said Brad.

'It's very close to Trafalgar Square. Sit back and enjoy it.'

As they sped towards London, Mr Chivers told them of other winners he had escorted in this way, some of them teetering on the edge of hysteria. Not all had lived happily ever after.

The office that he took them to in Cockspur Street seemed to be full of people. At its centre was a splendid desk, mahogany with satinwood inlay, and a large blue envelope was placed strategically in the middle of it. The man who had been sitting at the desk stood up when they came in. He was a big man with a red face and an expensive beige suit, and he made introductions to the other people there, although neither Brad nor Olivia, their heads filled with riches, would remember any names. There was a solicitor, a man from a bank, an accountant from the Camelot hierarchy, and two pretty girls, one of whom asked if they would like champagne.

'Tea is available,' said Mr Chivers. 'Some prefer it.'

'Coffee would be nice,' said Olivia. She had no wish to see her husband wandering off slightly drunk with a cheque for £11 million in his pocket.

There was an unreal atmosphere in the room created by the unreality of the situation. Where else did hired workers routinely hand out cheques for over £10 million to complete strangers? Mr Chivers hovered cheerfully in the background, a modern-day Robin Hood. Brad wondered whether he did the Lottery.

Olivia was overwhelmed by the courtesy and kindness of these money men. She sipped her coffee, laughed at their jokes and seemed to Brad to be assuming the persona of a rich woman as he watched. Having met people like this in his job, he adopted a more down-to-earth give-me-the-loot approach.

'Do I take the cheque with me?' he asked. He had been there ten minutes and not seen any money at all.

'We don't recommend it,' said the man in the beige suit. 'But you can have a look at it.' He picked up the blue envelope from the desk with a theatrical flourish and handed it to Brad. He opened it, glanced at the cheque as if this was a daily event, and passed it to Olivia.

'And here's a photocopy of it for you to keep as a souvenir!' Another envelope was passed to Brad, as the man explained that the money would be transferred to his bank account today, and there was no need for Brad to take the cheque home. The account would be set up in a private arm of his own bank, in Brad's case Coutts. This discreet method of handling the matter would prevent gossip seeping from his own bank at home.

'How do you feel about publicity?' Mr Chivers asked.

'We're against it,' said Olivia firmly.

'Fair enough,' said the man in the suit. 'Now let me tell you about some of our services. In a couple of weeks, when you've had time to think about it, you can seek the help, if you want it, of our financial panel.'

Olivia didn't feel that she needed any advice on how to spend money, but Brad made some notes and then had a long talk to the man from the bank. An hour later they were driven home in a daze.

Olivia stared out of the window, not seeing the raucous traffic that fought for every inch of space. She was being fawned over by beautiful men in the world's best couturiers, selecting and rejecting show-stopping ball gowns, slip dresses in satin and silk, and the latest creations from Galliano.

Brad's eyes were shut. He already knew what he was going to do with at least some of his money.

He could now afford to buy people!

9

Olivia Rowe, millionairess, went through Harrods like a marauding army. When the haul was completed it needed a shiny green Harrods van to deliver the stuff to her door: shoes and clothes, including a fleece kaftan, a buffalo leather bag with deerhorn handles, a Prada bag and a Louis Vuitton bag, bedding and furniture, including a six-foot hallstand, and an elaborate chandelier. 'We need a new house,' she said.

A million pounds had been put in her own account and Brad was curious to see what would be left after twelve months.

The Audi — a 1.8 cabriolet in orinoco green with platinum leather — had been almost given away to the ferret-eyed car dealer who praised her legs, and been replaced by a new maroon Mercedes SL500 which had a plasma television screen and a satellite navigational instrument which told you the correct next turning no matter where you were.

Brad's first purchase was less extravagant. The pounding heart and the breathlessness which had accompanied his lonely celebration of the win provided an unwelcome reminder that his sojourn on this planet was not as open ended as he had idly hoped. He was gripped by a sense of parts seizing up, fuel running out and wheels coming off. A future of infirmity and decrepitude beckoned. He devised a vitamin-rich diet and bought an exercise bike.

This acquisition amused Olivia, who had not previously associated him with unnecessary physical activity of any kind. Jobs that could not be accomplished without the assistance of a remote control device were somehow overlooked or farmed out to those practitioners of the black economy who would do almost anything for you if you paid them in cash.

Brad pedalled zealously for a week before incurring a pain in the peroneal nerve which confirmed in him his distaste for non-essential exercise. He limped for days and looked forward to that moment when sloth and indolence would restore him to the peak of fitness he had known before his impetuous purchase.

He bought himself a car. It was a silver-pearl Rolls-Royce Corniche which cost him a quarter of a million pounds. Looking at the legendary Spirit of Ecstasy emblem in his garage he felt that it was money well spent.

His reluctance to go out faded with the

arrival of this new toy. He went for a drive every morning with no destination in mind. He would end up beside the Thames, or up in the Chiltern Hills, but never got out of the car. The pleasure was in the driving.

'You're like a boy with a new bike,' Olivia told him. 'At least when I get in the Merc I'm going somewhere.'

'Yes. Shopping,' said Brad.

He had a fear of leaving the car in a deserted public place where it would become an instant target for the vandals as the Bentley had been. In car parks, which seemed to provide many drivers with their most difficult challenge, it would be bumped and scraped. Parked at the side of the road the car was prey to a dozen disasters, particularly the pedals of cyclists, pushed into too little space by passing lorries. The Spirit of Ecstasy emblem was something that fascinated thieves.

It dawned on him belatedly that a Rolls-Royce Corniche created envy, and envious people did not behave well. The pleasure the car gave him was counterbalanced by the worries it created. He anguished over the dilemma for three days and then bought a Volkswagen Passat. The Corniche would stay under wraps in the garage and be used on suitable occasions; the Passat would

94

transport him to the supermarket and on other mundane excursions that were part of the provincial quotidian.

Olivia, who had approved of the Corniche because it would impress her friends, was dismayed at the appearance of the Passat.

'What did you want to buy that for?' she asked. 'I'm not riding in it.'

'It'll take me to the shops and the supermarket and the pub,' he told her. 'The Corniche is a bit out of place for trips like that.'

She was reading a fashion magazine in the conservatory, and fingering one of her recent trophies, an eighteen-carat gold pendant necklace from Bulgari that cost £900. 'I thought the next time you wrote a cheque it might pay for a holiday,' she said. 'What about St Moritz in February? Everybody goes skiing then. The only travelling we seem to do is round supermarkets.'

'I know,' said Brad. 'I'm a sort of Tesco da Gama, aren't I?'

He smiled at his little joke which his wife missed. He hated skiing and had bigger purchases in mind.

★ ★ ★

In a meadow not half a mile away — after what were widely presumed to have been some astutely placed backhanders — planning permission had been granted for six luxury homes. Each had half an acre of ground which would provide plenty of space for the blue swimming pool and red tennis court that would undoubtedly follow.

When Brad appeared in the middle of this lavish development in the Corniche — deliberately chosen for the mission — a young salesman with a blond quiff shot out of the temporary mobile office like a greyhound from the traps.

'Good afternoon, sir,' he said. 'Can I show you round?'

Brad nodded. If he had turned up in the Passat the salesman would probably still be sitting in his little office, smoking a leisurely Silk Cut.

But Brad almost welcomed the company. Driving here, he had thought that one of the saddest things about his professional disaster was that not one of his former employees had been in touch with him since. Of course they had all lost their jobs and been plunged into a financial nightmare, but he had thought that they were friends and not just employees. Obviously Clive and Andy were the only real friends he had.

'We've sold number six already,' said the salesman, pointing at a house at the end. 'A chap came in and bought it when it was half built. But we haven't put this development on the market yet. We want customers to see the finished thing.'

The only thing that didn't seem to be finished were the drives. Two men were working on them now, laying red bricks in a neat herringbone pattern.

Each home had six bedrooms, three with ensuite bathrooms, and, outside, a triple garage with direct access to the house. The salesman pointed this out as he unlocked the door to number one and ushered Brad in.

Brad thought that he lived in a large house but this one seemed to have twice the space. He was immediately confronted by a huge hall with many doors leading from it.

'Under-floor heating,' said the salesman, tapping the floor with his heel. He led him into a large dining room with views of the garden, and then to something called the family room which was probably intended to have a large-screen television. Double doors took them through to a big drawing room with beautiful arched windows at one end, and then they went back to the other end of the house to a hand-built oak kitchen with limestone and oak flooring.

Aware of the salesman's eye, looking for his approval, Brad just nodded solemnly as the house's virtues were drawn to his attention.

'In Surrey this would be a million pound house,' the salesman told him.

'And here?' said Brad.

'Six hundred, give or take fifty quid. Of course they'll be worth a million in five years' time.'

'Why don't you wait and sell it in five years then?' Brad asked.

'Too many other projects on the go, sir. Now, have a look at the utility room, and then I'll show you the study and games room. There's also a downstairs cloakroom and toilet. Are you looking to sell a house?'

'No,' said Brad. He was astonished at how much space there was. Every room was larger than he expected. The salesman led him into the games room, which was big enough to house two snooker tables.

'Do you play snooker, sir?' the salesman asked.

Despite being impressed, Brad couldn't help disliking salesmen. Their friendship was false, their truths were questionable, and their sole motivation was to separate him from his money. But this eager young man, with his silly quiff and bogus affability, had something that Brad wanted.

'It's been known,' he grunted.

The salesman was now heading up the

solid oak staircase towards a dramatically beamed first floor. Brad followed less quickly: the pain inflicted by the exercise bike hadn't entirely gone. He glanced from an upstairs window and saw beyond the precious half-acre wooded countryside stretching into the distance under a winter sky. It always baffled him when people talked about this crowded island: you only had to fly over it to see that it was almost empty.

He went from bedroom to bedroom and examined the little bathrooms that were attached to each. The big rooms, with built-in wardrobes, looked cheerless empty, but properly furnished would rival the best hotels.

'What do you think?' the salesman asked. He was running out of material to impress his customer. 'There are two more bathrooms up here for the other three bedrooms.'

'It's good,' Brad conceded.

They went downstairs and out into the drive where the workmen were laying bricks.

'Can I look at the others?' Brad asked.

'You can do, but they're identical,' said the salesman.

Brad shook his head. 'I won't bother then.' He was waiting for the man to make an impassioned sales pitch, but no speech was forthcoming. Selling houses wasn't like selling anything else. People went away and thought about it. In fact, the salesman was now extending his hand in a farewell gesture.

'Don't you want to know whether I'm going to buy a house?' Brad asked him.

The salesman paused. 'Well, naturally, if you're that far down the road . . . '

Brad pulled out his Coutts cheque book and pointed at number 1, number 2 and number 3. 'I'll have that one, that one and that one,' he said.

10

In these crepuscular days, Clive Preston became accustomed to hostility on all sides, but the assault that he faced from his daughter one morning was outside anything that he could have anticipated.

The family's new home, a three-bedroom semi-detached which cost not much more than half what they had been paid for their former house, was a bleak building that looked as if it had been thrown up in a Depression; the bare grey concrete frontage suggested that austerity had been the guiding hand in the builder's office. The furniture it couldn't accommodate was packed away in the garage, and the BMW was parked permanently in the muddy drive. The view from the rear windows, of a huge cemetery, was never going to lift spirits that were already on the floor, and to complete his misery Clive hadn't emerged from this humiliating relocation with as much money as he had hoped: he had still owed too much on the first mortgage.

Holly's reaction to the move seemed to be a dazed disbelief. She couldn't understand how all the work and planning had dumped her in these insalubrious surroundings. She moved round the house — cooking, cleaning, ironing — in a sort of trance and never smiled.

In this mood one afternoon she found her demoralized husband's lanky frame stretched out on the sofa as he listened with a pained heart to Mahler's Fifth Symphony. If music was the brandy of the damned, he decided, it was an appropriate refreshment.

Holly sat on the edge of the sofa, a strong enough hint for him to turn off the music.

'Have you done anything about getting a job?' she asked.

Clive's mood darkened at the thought. He wanted work, but knew only too well that among those circles where his sort of job existed he would already be a joke for his performance on the desk. Who would take him seriously now?

'I'm biding my time,' he said.

'You haven't got any time to bide,' said Holly. 'We need money to get out of this rat-hole.'

'I'm waiting for the right job to come up, darling,' he suggested. 'I had a good position. I was business development and marketing manager of a big concern. Jobs like that don't come up every day, and why should I accept less?'

'Because we need the money,' she replied briskly.

Behind the blonde good looks there was a woman who knew exactly what she wanted, and what she wanted was an orderly and comfortable life. She wasn't greedy — she had never developed a taste for the extravagant baubles that evidently sustained the rich, but poverty and privation weren't on her list either.

'If you don't get a move on,' she said, 'you'll be out of touch or too old.'

'I *am* old. I can remember when paedophiles were called child molesters.'

But she was not to be diverted.

'You've got to forget this supposedly triumphant past, and take what you can get. This isn't a house I want to live in for very long.'

'I'll make some phone calls.'

'Knock hard,' she said. 'Life is deaf.'

He watched her march out of the room and wondered, What happened to the jasmine-scented landscape of love?

★   ★   ★

The following morning he sat in a bedroom upstairs where he could use a phone in peace. In front of him was a list of contacts in the world where he had once earned a good living. They were all necessarily former rivals who had felt the heat of his competitive nature, and some of them had probably rejoiced at his downfall. But good manners prevailed. It was not unusual in the ever-changing world of business for yesterday's enemy to become today's ally, and Clive Preston had once been big enough to command respect.

But the superficial courtesy could not disguise the fact that nobody was offering him a job. The problem was that the people he approached saw him as a rival if he joined their firm. They all suggested other places he might try, but when he did they suggested the firm that had suggested them. Clive spent an hour on this whirligig before realizing that a personal appearance and an invitation to lunch might produce more positive results. His only consolation was that nobody had mentioned the desk.

As he dropped the phone on the bed in exasperation, his daughter appeared at the door.

'Hallo, dear,' he said.

She was wearing a black leather mini-skirt over which hung a white T-shirt bearing in blue letters the message WE LOVE ROBBIE. The third new hairstyle this week featured a few plaited strands hanging down over each cheek. Her expression, he was alarmed to see, combined hatred and contempt.

'I've got your number, Dad,' she said, and sat on the bed. Her pale face, Clive thought, suggested either inner tension or an unhealthy lifestyle.

'My number?' he asked.

'I know what you've been up to. I know why you were sacked.'

The initial lurch in his stomach was swiftly quelled. She couldn't possibly know why he was sacked.

'I told you about my redundancy, Charlotte. These things happen in business, I'm afraid.' Even as he said it, she was giving him a funny look.

'I know what happens in business,' she said. 'Tarts get bonked on desks.'

Now he was seriously frightened, and groped for the words that would subdue her.

'I don't know what you're talking about, Charlotte, but I don't like your language.'

'Bonked. Shagged. Screwed. I'm talking English, aren't I?' She had been gazing at the floor, but now turned to face him. 'You and the cleaning lady.'

Clive's main concern now was that Holly would hear.

'Keep your voice down,' he said. 'You're talking English, but only a moron's version of it.'

'Well, we're talking about a moron's behaviour,' she replied quickly.

He looked at her in horror. How could this girl, reared in a loving environment, be so hard? What produced this raw hatred? He sat on the bed with her. 'Where did this silly story come from?' he asked.

Charlotte didn't look at him. Television, videos, newspapers and conversations at school had persuaded her in the last year that there was more to life than the boring middle-class existence that satisfied her parents, and the almost furtive shift into a smaller, nastier house convinced her that she had the wrong parents, that she had been born into the wrong family and that she would be better off somewhere else.

She said: 'A girl at school's father works for your old firm, and she heard him telling her mother the story. She heard the name and asked me if it was you. She was having a laugh because she didn't even know you worked there — I never talk about you. But I knew straight away that it *was* you. How many people called Preston could they have fired in the last month?'

The comprehensive nature of the reply numbed him, but the phrase 'damage limitation' drifted into his head.

'If you tell this nonsense to your mother

you'll upset her greatly,' he said.

'And then she'll upset you.' She stood up. 'What about this Robbie Williams CD?'

He fished a £20 note from his wallet and handed it to her. Was he now being blackmailed by his own daughter?

He left her in the bedroom and went downstairs, fearful that Holly had heard some of this. The morning's post was on the front-door mat. He picked it up and went through to the kitchen.

'Phoned anybody?' said Holly, who was ironing some of Charlotte's clothes. This was not a question that he wanted to hear, but it was welcome now: it meant that she hadn't heard the conversation upstairs.

'A lot of people,' he said, 'but none of them have any helpful suggestions.'

'So what are you going to do?'

'I'll have to start taking people out to lunch. It's how things happen these days, I'm afraid. Phone calls are a waste of time.'

His mind was still filled with the conversation with his daughter, and the thought came to him now that her unpleasant behaviour had been caused by drugs. The papers gave you the impression that half of today's teenagers floundered around in a haze of crack and smack, and Charlotte had already revealed an appetite for the forbidden. He needed to nail her, to grill her, to find out the truth. But he was wary of her now, with her secret knowledge and aggressive nature. She had the status of an unexploded bomb.

He flipped through the post on the table, most of it redirected Christmas cards. One envelope, larger than the others, stood out, and he recognized Brad's handwriting. He opened it immediately. There was no card, but a large sheet of Brad's old agency's notepaper with a message scribbled over the whole page in large black writing.

Mr and Mrs Preston (and Charlotte) are invited to drink champagne at 11 am on Sunday, December 23, with Mr and Mrs Rowe. A chauffeur-driven car will call for you at that hour. Attendance is compulsory. There is a present for you.

The pseudo-formality of the message puzzled him. If Brad had information to convey he picked up a phone. In fact, apart from a couple of postcards from faraway places, he couldn't remember receiving a handwritten communication from him before. He passed the invitation to Holly, who put down her iron to read it. 'I suppose this means we've got to buy a present for them,' she said.

11

Despite his many achievements, what is Sir Walter Raleigh most famous for? For draping his cloak over a puddle to protect the Queen's feet. When Clare pointed this out to her preoccupied husband, he felt like the referee who had forgotten to bring the ball. Walter Raleigh without the cloak was like George Washington without the cherry tree, or William Tell without the apple.

Andy agonized for two hours over this omission from his manuscript, which was now almost finished. He had spent a lot of time researching Raleigh's story, and had recently discovered that his son, Carew, lived in a Jacobean mansion in Surrey, and had buried his father's severed head in West Horsley church. But the secret of success here, he decided, was knowing what to leave out. The story had to be told in a clear, straightforward sequence, uncluttered by extraneous incidents. Carew and the cloak were reluctantly consigned to the bin.

Whether the play was almost completed or actually finished was another problem at this late stage. Andy found that you could fiddle with words on paper almost interminably and never let them go. Oscar Wilde could spend all morning deciding to insert a comma, and then, after an afternoon's thought, decide to take it out again, and Andy knew how he felt. He read the play over and over, making small amendments here and there, but when he could read it through without making any alterations at all he began to wonder seriously whether it was finished.

'What are you going to do with it now?' asked Clare one evening, after a busy day at the delicatessen.

It was a question that Andy had never faced. What did you do with a play? You could hardly send it to theatres which, with touring companies, West End try-outs, and one-off rock concerts, were never occupied by the same people from one week to the next.

'I dunno,' he muttered. 'I can't remember why I started it now. How do you sell a play?'

'What about Warren Goldberg?' Clare asked.

Andy's first (and last) novel, *Raging Hormones*, had appeared to a burst of critical applause ('I laughed and I laughed' — Auberon Waugh) fifteen years ago when he was twenty-four. The warmth of the reception had persuaded him to embark on another, about a flurry of adulterous relationships destroying the harmonious balance of a bridge club in Penge, but he couldn't make the imaginative leaps which the scenario demanded and the novel was never finished.

This failure was a cruel disappointment to Warren Goldberg, the agent whose name Andy had plucked from a writers' directory, and who saw in Andy, once he had read the typed manuscript of *Raging Hormones*, a future big earner. Writers came and went, of course, but they usually stayed longer than this.

For a year or two he would send Andy sad little cards reminding him of his success and asking hopefully what was 'in the works'; but when this gentle prodding produced nothing, the cards stopped.

Andy, not then accustomed to setbacks and failure, felt that he had let his agent down. Warren Goldberg had found a British publisher in a week and an American publisher in under a month. He was a man of great determination and knowledge who knew how to push a career, and Andy had left him with an empty gun. When he succumbed to Clare's coaxing and picked up his newly installed phone to ring Warren Goldberg Ltd, he was filled with guilt.

A lady with more energy than the usual phone-answer said briskly, 'Warren Goldberg Ltd.'

'Could I speak to Mr Goldberg?' Andy asked.

'He's on the other line at the moment.'

'I'll call back,' Andy said, suddenly feeling the need for time to assemble his thoughts.

'Who's calling?'

'Devlin. Andy Devlin.'

A strange hiss came down the line which wasn't explained. 'Would that be the author of *Raging Hormones*?'

Andy was embarrassed. Fifteen years was a long time ago. 'I wrote it, yes,' he admitted.

'I read it at school. It's one of my favourite novels,' the lady said. 'Listen, don't hang up. Warren would love to talk to you. I'm Maureen, his secretary, by the way.'

'Hallo,' said Andy. 'I'll hang on.'

He was sitting at his desk in the smallest bedroom with the bulky manuscript of his play in front of him. The telephone was not his favorite method of communicating. If a face-to-face meeting wasn't possible, he preferred letters. But Clare had told him that this was a case for the phone, and he sat there wondering what Warren Goldberg was like these days after fifteen more years of chasing deals, pushing books and twisting the arms of wavering publishers.

He was a short, plump man who seemed to have more hair in his ears than on his head, and he never stopped moving. Tucked away in this bouncing ball of energy and enthusiasm was great literary judgement and a sharp commercial instinct. Occasionally, in predatory mood, he had poached an author from a rival agency and the author, according to the gossip that Andy read in the Sunday book pages, found his income trebled.

'Andy!' a throaty voice shouted suddenly in his ear. 'How are you?'

Andy felt plunged into the past. 'Warren, I'm fine. How are *you*?'

'We're surviving out here in Red Lion Square. It doesn't get any easier, does it?' Warren's picture of the agent's life had always been painted in sombre colours, but he was reputed to own one of the biggest houses in Hampstead. 'Of course, it would be a lot easier if our writers wrote. Who do you think you are? Salinger?'

Andy fingered the manuscript in front of him. It wasn't the sort of thing Warren Goldberg would want or expect. 'I've just finished writing something,' he said diffidently.

'Something? What is it? A love letter? A sonnet? An advertising jingle?'

'It's a play,' Andy admitted.

'A play?'

'Do you handle such things?'

'Novels, plays, poetry, suicide notes. You name it, we handle it.'

'Suicide notes?'

'I've just sold a book of them. Fascinating reading, actually. What's the play about?'

'Walter Raleigh.'

'A curiously neglected figure.'

'That's what I thought.'

'Send it to me, Andy. I look forward to it. Christmas is buggering up the post, but I'll get it eventually. And listen — great to hear from you.'

Warren wanted to be off. There was probably a call on the other line. Andy replaced the phone and began a long and eventually successful search of the drawers in his desk for a padded envelope which would accommodate his play.

He took Greg to the post office with him as Clare was at work. He didn't want to go, but he didn't want to be left alone in the house either.

'Life's full of difficult choices,' Andy told him. 'What do you want for Christmas?'

'A bike,' Greg replied instantly.

A bike was the last thing that Andy wanted to buy him. The road outside the house was a racetrack where even pedestrians felt threatened. All attempts to introduce a speed limit had apparently crumbled against the stone wall of local bureacracy.

'We'll see,' Andy said.

When they got home, the doormat was covered with Christmas cards. The change-of-address cards which Clare had diligently sent out were producing dividends. Andy scooped them up and found that one envelope was larger than the others. He also recognized the writing, which came as a surprise. Brad didn't normally send them Christmas cards.

'I never send Christmas cards,' he said once, 'because they only encourage people.' But Andy knew that when his firm was running he dispatched hundreds, often with presents, to sweeten his clients and people he hoped would become clients. Probably by the time he got home from work he was sick of the whole idea.

He made himself a coffee and sat down in the kitchen with the post. Greg had gone off in search of a suitably lurid video. The envelope that bore Brad's flamboyant hand-writing, inscribed, by the look of it, with a black rollerball pen, contained no Christmas card. Instead there was a single sheet of Bradley Rowe Images notepaper with the name of the defunct enterprise scored through with two black lines. The large writing of the message filled the page.

* * *

Mr and Mrs Devlin (and Greg) are invited to drink champagne at 11am on Sunday, December 23, with Mr and Mrs Rowe. A chauffeur-driven car will call for you at that hour. Attendance is compulsory. There is a present for you.

* * *

Mystified, he laid the note on the table. His first impulse was to phone Brad, but after some thought he felt that this violated the spirit of the invitation. Mystery was part of the programme.

He looked through the other cards — from Australia, Ibiza, Hong Kong and Canada — and marvelled at the way people had casually put half a world between themselves and their roots when he found it a financial challenge to get to London.

12

Standing expectantly at the window, waiting for the mysterious chauffeur-driven car, Andy, Clare and Greg were surprised and impressed when a silver-pearl Rolls-Royce Corniche glided to a halt at their gate. At the wheel was a burly driver wearing a black peaked cap.

'Wicked!' said Greg. 'It's a Roller!'

'A taste of luxury at last,' said Clare. 'Let's go.' She was carrying a video of *Chicago*, a present for Brad and Olivia, and, intimidated by Olivia's fancy couture had put on her best pale blue two-piece.

They stepped out of the house, admiring the sleek lines of the transport that had been provided, and it was only when the chauffeur emerged to open their door that they realized it was Brad.

'Good morning, people,' he said. 'Please make yourselves comfortable.'

They climbed into the back, intrigued by this development. The smell of new leather filled their nostrils.

'You didn't have to hire a Rolls to fetch us,' Andy said. 'We're quite happy in a Mondeo.'

'My husband speaks for himself,' Clare said. 'I find this vehicle entirely suitable.' She sat back in her seat, enjoying the luxurious comfort of it.

'I've never been in a Rolls before,' said Greg, staring fascinated at the dashboard.

The car pulled silently away. They hadn't even realized that the engine was running.

'What's this all about, Brad?' Andy asked. 'You're moving in mysterious ways.'

'All will become clear,' said Brad. 'First we have to pick up the Prestons if I can find their new home.'

Clive and Holly were standing outside a drab, grey house with a small neglected front garden. Behind it was a large cemetery. An uneasy truce prevailed between them as they faced the prospect of a rare social occasion together.

'I knew it would be late,' Holly was saying.

'Here it is,' said Clive. 'God, it's a Rolls.'

Brad stuck his head out of the window. 'Holly, come in the front. There's plenty of room for Clive in the back. Where's Charlotte?'

'She wouldn't come,' said Holly. 'She's having one of her moods. I thought you were a chauffeur in that cap.'

'I am a chauffeur,' said Brad. 'Do get in.'

Clive got in the back. It was surprising how

much room there was. 'What's going on?' he asked.

'Buggered if I know,' said Andy. 'Nice wheels, though.'

They drove back to the area where they had all recently lived. The low December sun was in their eyes and Brad pulled down the peak of his cap. Bare trees lined the almost empty roads.

'I feel I should wave to people,' said Holly, 'but there's nobody to wave to.'

'They're all indoors wrapping their Christmas presents,' said Brad. 'You get a lot of that sort of thing at this time of the year.'

'I have your present here,' said Holly, producing a video of *Chicago* from her bag. 'Olivia will love it.'

Clive stared mournfully out of the window. Recent events had not equipped him for cheerful appearances at social gatherings, which demanded a geniality and *joie de vivre* that he couldn't quite manage.

'You're getting a bit flamboyant for somebody whose business has just gone down the pan, aren't you?' he asked sourly. 'What did it cost to hire this motor?'

'I've no idea,' Brad replied cheerfully. 'I didn't hire it.' He took a turn that none of them had expected.

'Where are we going?' Andy asked. 'I

thought we were heading for your house?'

'We are,' Brad assured him.

The unanswered questions were left to hang in the air as they turned into a small enclave of luxurious new homes. Brad drove past the first few, which were all empty, and pulled into the wide drive of number I, where curtains in the windows and smoke from the chimney suggested occupation. One door of an impressive triple garage was open, revealing a new maroon Mercedes. Some of the questions which arrived now were answered when Olivia opened the front door holding a bottle of champagne.

'Brad,' said Andy, 'is there something you haven't told us?'

'Quite a lot,' Brad said, getting out of the car and removing his chauffeur's cap. 'Welcome to my new home. And by the way, the car's mine.' He ignored their confusion and marched towards Olivia while the others followed, exchanging baffled glances. A flurry of air-kissing greeted them on the doorstep.

'I haven't seen you for ages, Clare,' said Olivia. 'How's the new house?'

'Bloody horrible, thanks,' said Clare. 'I prefer this one.' She produced the video. 'We bought you a present, but it seems that Holly has chosen the same one.'

'That's all right,' said Olivia, leading them

in. 'I promised to get one for my sister.'

She began to pour the champagne while they looked round the room. Everything in it was new — the dusty-pink carpets, the furniture, the new red glass chandelier that hung over this opulence, a silver mirror hanging above the roaring fire.

'What will you drink, Greg?' Brad asked.

Greg was staring round the room in wonderment.

'Do you have coke?'

'There's some bought specially for you in the kitchen. Come with me and I'll show you my snooker table.'

Brad was wearing a new double-breasted blazer — an image change. He put his hand on the boy's shoulder and led him from the room in a way that made Andy wonder whether he wished he had children.

Olivia was lacquering a six-foot Christmas tree in the corner of the room, and talking to Clare and Holly, who had been enviously studying the new four-seater sofa.

'How's Clive taking redundancy?' Olivia asked.

Holly grimaced. 'I think he's fading away. He's so unobtrusive these days that even the automatic doors in supermarkets don't register his presence. They keep slamming

121

shut in his face. It tells you something, doesn't it?'

'Can't he get another job?'

'I've recommended suicide bomber, but he lacks the mechanical know-how apparently.'

Andy and Clive were standing in the middle of the room with their drinks, bewildered by this transformation in the Rowe family's fortunes. Clive looked as if he wasn't quite sure why he was there, like a spider in a bath.

'What do you make of it?' he asked.

'I'm waiting for an explanation,' said Andy. He called to Olivia: 'What have you done with the other house?'

'Brad's left tenants there,' said Olivia.

'My God, has he got a lieutenant as well?'

'Your jokes don't get any better, Andy,' said Olivia disdainfully. She rarely laughed.

When Brad returned he insisted on giving them a tour of the house. Not all the rooms were furnished yet, but those that were exuded luxury.

'The house is bigger than it looks,' said Clare.

'Exactly,' said Brad. 'Do you like it?'

'It's wonderful,' Clare said sadly.

'Let's go downstairs. I've got a present for you.'

'You mentioned that on your invitation.'

'Here it comes,' said Brad.

Downstairs he refilled all their glasses and then took the centre of the room. He raised a hand to silence his wife, who was explaining to Holly that the picture on her car's television disappeared for safety reasons when the car was in motion.

'Ladies and gentlemen,' Brad said. 'As it's Christmas, I have bought you presents. One for the Devlins, one for the Prestons.'

Warming himself by the fire, Andy wondered what sort of present could justify this portentous build-up. Presents, in his experience, were passed over in a much more self-effacing manner.

'The only question,' Brad went on, 'is who gets which present? I've decided that the matter will be resolved by the toss of a coin.'

'I'll get the electric toothbrush,' said Andy. 'I never have any luck with tossed coins.'

Brad had already produced a fifty-pence coin from his pocket. He spun it into the air, caught it, and slapped it on the back of his hand. Andy and Clive looked at each other, waiting for the other to call.

Clive eventually broke the silence. 'Tails,' he said.

Brad looked at the coin and showed it to them. 'It's tails.'

'I knew it,' said Andy. 'I couldn't back the

winner in a walkover.'

But now they were all looking at Brad, waiting for the production of these much-heralded presents. He returned the coin to his pocket, and rubbed his hands together in an expression of imminent pleasure.

'You all have to come outside,' he announced.

'Outside?' said Andy. 'I've won the bloody wheelbarrow, haven't I?'

They filed obediently out of the house and seemed at first to be heading for the triple garage. But Brad marched past this and ended up on the drive of the house next door. He pointed at the house, and then at the next one.

'You won the toss, Clive. Do you want number 2 or number 3?'

Clive stared at him. He wasn't in the mood for jokes, but felt a guest's obligation to play along.

'Oh, I'll have number two,' he replied dutifully.

'Right,' said Brad. He pulled a key from his pocket and unlocked the front door. 'Come in. It's yours.' He handed the key to Clive.

Clive looked at Holly, who shrugged, as puzzled as he was. But Brad was in the house now and they all followed him in, awaiting an explanation.

'Very nice,' said Clive. 'It's like yours.'

'Identical,' said Brad. 'Andy, you get number 3.' He tossed him a key.

'It's a good game, Brad, but I don't quite get it,' Andy said, looking at the key. 'What's going on?'

'I've bought you both a house,' said Brad. 'I was missing you.'

'You've bought us both a house?' said Clare incredulously. 'What do you mean?'

'I've got the deeds in my office. They haven't been filled in, or whatever you do with deeds, because I didn't know who would own which house.'

'Is this a joke?' asked Holly. 'Because if it's a joke it's not all that funny.'

'No joke, sweetheart,' said Brad, putting his arm round her. 'You've got yourself a new home.'

Olivia stepped forward and gave Holly a hug. 'It's true, kid. You own the house. Brad's bought it for you. And you, Clare.'

Clare looked confused. 'I think I'm losing the plot,' she said.

Clive took Andy's arm. 'Are you believing any of this?' he asked quietly.

'None of it,' Andy told him. 'But it's fun to imagine. Would you like to see my place?' He was clutching the key that Brad had thrown to him, and he led the others out to number

3. He was faintly surprised when the key opened the door. They all walked into the empty house with its bare floors and curtainless windows, and tried to imagine it furnished. Greg, untouched by the pervasive scepticism, broke away from the group and went off to find his own room.

When the party drifted back to Brad's house for more champagne, a mood of silent bemusement had descended on it. Holly and Clare, reassured by Olivia, were beginning to believe that they had suddenly acquired wonderful new homes, but didn't dare say so in case they looked foolish. Andy and Clive, on whom the ways of the world had bestowed a cheerful cynicism, could not overlook Brad's capacity for deception. They still suspected a joke, although they could see nothing that deserved a laugh.

By the time they sat down with their drinks, Brad had been upstairs and returned with two large brown envelopes. He sat on the sofa, the envelopes on his lap.

'I have the feeling that you guys don't believe me,' he said. 'I'm driven to this conclusion by the fact that nobody has said thank you.'

'That's true,' said Clive, looking embarrassed. 'The fact is, it's too incredible to believe.'

'But it's true, Clive,' Olivia exclaimed. 'Brad wants all his little friends around him. All boys together.'

Andy gave her a quick look. He detected a hint that even if this amazing thing had actually happened, and the houses were theirs, Olivia didn't entirely approve of the purchase. Another thought struck him.

'Even were it to be true,' he said, 'there are other factors that float into your mind. What does it cost, for instance, to live in a house like this? We can hardly pay the expenses on the slum we've got now.'

Brad smiled broadly. 'I've thought of that,' he said. 'The answer and the deeds are in the envelope.' He handed one each to Andy and Clive. 'Have a look.'

Andy opened the envelope and pulled out a large document which he saw was the deeds of the house.

'There's something else in there,' Brad told him.

Andy peered into the envelope. There was a piece of paper at the bottom and he pulled it out. It was a cheque for £500,000.

'Christ!' he said, and passed it to his wife. But his reaction, he found, was that the cheque confirmed his suspicion that this was an elaborate and seemingly pointless hoax. The cheque was a step too far.

Clive, who had withdrawn a cheque for the same amount from his envelope, had evidently been pushed in the same direction.

'I'm more confused than ever now, Brad,' he said, showing Holly the cheque. 'Are you going to explain?'

'I will explain,' said Brad, 'but you must treat what I tell you in confidence.'

'You've robbed a bank,' said Clare. 'Your secret's safe with us.'

'As good as,' Brad told her. 'I won eleven million on the Lottery.'

The relief in the room was sensational. Suddenly it all made sense. The houses were real. The half million was real. The room exploded. People were on their feet, hugging each other, shaking hands, and, in Clare and Holly's cases, kissing Brad.

'Bloody fantastic!' Andy shouted, hugging Olivia who wasn't entirely at ease with such public emotion. Clive, showing his first genuine smile in weeks, was kissing Clare on the cheek.

Brad stood there watching this spontaneous outpouring of love with huge satisfaction. His friends had found little to smile at lately, but suddenly here was pure joy. Andy was striding round the room repeating, 'bloody fantastic!' Clive was rubbing his face and muttering, 'I can't believe it.' The women were laughing as they contemplated the new homes they were going to create.

'Does this mean I can have a bike for Christmas?' Greg asked.

'And a computer,' Clare told him, giving him a kiss and a hug.

Brad, smiling permanently now, was opening another bottle of champagne.

★   ★   ★

'Can we accept it?' Clare asked, as they lay in bed that night. She asked the question dispassionately despite the fact that Andy was nibbling her thigh.

His head appeared from the duvet. 'Of course we can accept it. A starving man takes what he's given.' He felt more relaxed than he had for months.

'It's an odd situation though,' she said.

He pulled himself up the bed. 'Enjoy it,' he said. 'God knows, you deserve a break. Tomorrow's Christmas Eve. I'll put the cheque in the bank first thing, and then you can go out and spend what you want. I'll get Greg a computer. The bike can wait until we move to the safer surroundings of our new home.'

'And when will that be?'

'As soon as possible. We can choose carpets

tomorrow, and I'll talk to the removal people. I wonder if they work on the 27th?'

He was anxious to be off. A brighter life would start when they had moved. There was a new world waiting.

★   ★   ★

In the Preston household there was an unfamiliar atmosphere of hope. Holly, temporarily mollified by the promised improvement in her recently damaged lifestyle, was even prepared to overlook the fact that it owed nothing to her husband. Her mind was on other things. The Caribbean cruise was back on her agenda.

But Clive, delighted as he was by this strange shift in his fortunes, could not pretend that his problems were over. The first reminder of this came when a Christmas card arrived from Sandra. Luckily he was sifting through the mail that morning and found it before Holly could see it and ask questions. But its sudden appearance made him feel vulnerable and exposed.

The picture showed a muscular and cheerful Santa Claus delivering Viagra. The message inside said 'With love from Sandra'. It frightened him more than he would have expected. He didn't even know that she had his address, particularly as he had moved since he left the office. She knew where he was and could reach him! He tried to reassure himself that his second house move would throw her off the track.

The second reminder came when Charlotte asked for a considerable increase in her weekly pocket money. He had hoped that the prospect of a wonderful new home would blunt her abrasive edge and bring back the lovely character he had once known. But she had talked to her mother and knew about the cheque.

She cornered him in the muddy drive where Clive was washing the BMW before looking for a buyer. It was to be replaced, as soon as they moved, by two new cars.

'Fifty pounds a week!' he exclaimed when Charlotte told him the new figure she had in mind. 'What on earth does a girl of fifteen want with fifty quid a week?'

'It seems a fair figure given the size of your cheque,' she said tonelessly. Today she was wearing pale blue jeans, holed fashionably at the knee, and a black and white striped rugby shirt.

'But you don't *need* that much, Charlotte!' he said.

She leaned on the car door and looked down at his bucket of dirty water.

'How's Sandra?' she asked.

This was doubly alarming: the last time they'd had a conversation like this she hadn't mentioned Sandra's name. He put down his sponge and looked at her.

He no longer knew anything about her; he didn't know what her life was like. Communication had broken down some time in the past when his questions suddenly became unwelcome. He had learned to respect her pubertal privacy. But who knew what she was up to now? In these fast-track days when no appetite was ignored, her virginity may already have gone. He could hardly bring himself to think about it. The menacing swarm of unwashed adolescents with their acne, their funny voices, their torn clothes and misguided lust could constitute a challenge to a rebellious fifteen-year-old that she might not be inclined to resist.

One minute he had been looking after her and the next she had removed herself from his care.

He wondered why she disliked him so much. The hate came off her like steam. It preceded the Sandra business, although the Sandra business hadn't helped.

Irritably conscious of the absurdity of it, but unable to see a strategic move, he said: 'OK, fifty quid a week.'

13

On the day after Boxing Day, two professionally packed removal lorries bearing the names
of rival firms arrived simultaneously in
Meadow Way. As they reversed into their
respective drives, exchanging amiable exple-
tives cab-to-cab, Andy and Clive were waiting
like recently installed lords of the manor to
greet them, having been dropped off by their
wives who had then returned to their old
homes to supervise the loading end of the
operation.

The removal men Andy was dealing with
— a stout middle-aged man and two burly
youngsters — were used to taking the
contents of a house from one end of the
country to the other, sleeping in the vehicle to
cut costs. The twenty-odd miles they were
travelling today was a welcome respite in a
gruelling schedule. Watching them work,
Andy wondered what the breakage rate was
on a job like this, but given the age and
cheapness of the family possessions it was
unlikely to become the subject of litigation.
Almost all of it, he guessed, would be
replaced in the next few months when the

truth about their windfall had sunk in.

'I'm not extravagant, but the house deserves it,' Clare had explained. Andy agreed with her. Their battered sofa would look incongruous in these bright new rooms. The kitchen furniture, second-hand when they bought it, would have to go.

Clare had the upper hand in these matters. She possessed talents that had escaped Andy. Two homes ago she had retiled the bathroom floor, painted the hall, and made a useful table with legs supplied from one store and wood and tiles bought in another. Diminished by these achievements, Andy retired to his typewriter and tapped out words that were intended to put food on the table. The sad fact that neither her formidable talent nor his produced money was overlooked in the creative swirl. But her artisan's skills would not be needed now that they could write cheques, and she was going to concentrate on colour and decoration.

The carpet men had arrived hours earlier and their work was almost done. With giant scissors and delicate hammers they worked on hands and knees, replacing bare boards with a cosy homeliness. Andy, redundant as ever, did a circuit of his new house, wondering how the rooms could be filled. The airy, open spaces had a refreshingly new smell, and the matt pink walls, not yet assaulted by pictures or mirrors, seemed to go on for ever. It was all beautifully silent. There were no moans from the plumbing or creaks from the floorboards. From the window he looked down on a field of sheep and, beyond it, a copse. The unearned prosperity that had suddenly propelled him to these Elysian heights from the subsistence level where he had spent most of his life made him feel dizzy. Unaccustomed to the amount of money that now languished in the wasteland that had been his bank account, he was unsure how to use it. But two cars were needed, and Clare's shopping list, which had once featured items like bread, sugar and eggs, was now headed by dishwasher, new microwave and fridge-freezer.

His bank manager, the scrupulous author of many a begging letter that had brought distress to the Devlin family in the past, assumed a cuddly new persona. He rang up like an old mate who wanted to borrow a video, and suggested a chat.

Over the phone he explained, as if to a child, that the money now lying in Andy's account would yield several hundred pounds a week in interest if invested wisely, and advice on such investments was available to his customers. Andy, unsure what would be left for investment after they had dealt with the growing shopping list, promised to get in touch.

The car he had his eye on was a Lotus Esprit GT3. He knew little about cars, but liked the low-slung look of it. Clare wanted a brand new Golf which was bigger than the Golf she had been driving for years, and Greg had some suggestions of his own. A satellite dish and a new large-screen television to accommodate the delights it would discharge topped his list. Andy was sorry to hear it. What rubbish would fill the boy's head now?

It had been a strange Christmas. Poised for flight, it had been difficult for them to celebrate in their cramped, rejected home. But Clare had bought a Christmas tree, a ritual Greg wouldn't allow them to ignore, and adorned it with last year's lights which twinkled through the dark December day.

Their minds were twenty miles away in the new home, and on the presents they would soon have, especially the cars. But for Greg they constructed a traditional Christmas, so that he awoke to find a pillowcase full of presents at the foot of his bed. The bike and the computer would arrive when they had moved, and he began to see the exercise as two Christmases rolled into one.

They sat in front of a roaring fire playing

one of the games that Greg had found among his presents. Andy had bought him a smart chess set but his son's tastes, rejecting the more austere disciplines of Andy's boyhood, lent towards the electronic.

Most of Boxing Day was spent packing, but the accompanying conversation was very cheerful. It involved words that they hadn't used much lately, like theatre, restaurants and travel.

★ ★ ★

For Clive's family, the move to a new home was a relatively simple matter. Much of their stuff was still packed from the previous move and had been lying in boxes in the garage. Holly's determination that their stay in what she called Cemetery Lane would be a short one had been triumphantly vindicated, and so had her refusal to unpack more than was necessary.

But as he stood in the hall, having paid off the removal men and the carpet layers, Clive wasn't expecting any smiles as he waited for Holly and Charlotte to arrive. Holly would march into the house and blame him for something that didn't meet with her approval: furniture in the wrong place, clothes not yet hung up, boxes still unopened. She would be feeling the stress of the day, and the tension would crackle.

Charlotte, who had never seen the house, would no doubt have her own poison to distribute. She saw gratitude these days as a weakness, and would probably find flaws in the new home that nobody else had noticed. And if the spleen deserted her, she would effortlessly produce a string of sarcastic remarks about who provided the money for all this. The articulateness that Clive had admired in her as a child had grown to be a weapon.

Waiting for their appearance, he felt upset that what should be a celebration would probably descend into a slanging match. He opened a can of beer and braced himself.

In fact, when they arrived they were laughing girlishly, probably at him. Increasingly these days he struck a mournful figure.

'Welcome to your new home,' he said with a smile.

'Daddy's been drinking,' said Charlotte, looking at the can of beer and nudging her mother.

'This isn't the sort of place where you stand on the doorstep with a can of beer in your hand,' said Holly. 'Also, your flies are undone.' They swept into the house, leaving him on the step.

'It's awesome, Mum!' said Charlotte, looking at the big rooms with their space and light.

'Wait till you see the kitchen!'

'I don't do kitchens,' Charlotte said. 'Which is my room?'

They went upstairs where Charlotte relayed, on a mobile phone she had been given for Christmas, a glowing commentary on the house to a friend. 'The rooms are, like, huge, and I've got my own bathroom,' she reported happily. 'Wicked or what?'

Holly, relieved at these rare signals of satisfaction from her usually disgruntled daughter went downstairs again. Clive was unpacking crockery.

'It's lovely,' she said. 'Of course we'll have to spend some money on things.'

'We seem to have some,' Clive replied.

'Thank you, Brad.'

While her parents unpacked boxes and filled cupboards, Charlotte set to work in the third en-suite bedroom (the second was to be reserved for guests) and in a matter of hours created her own Valhalla of darkened windows, cacophonous music, garish posters of a grunge-rock icon, currently in jail, and enough cosmetics to open a shop. It was a suitable home, Clive thought, for somebody who seemed to secrete a toxic venom, but

Holly, a loyal mother, told him that he shouldn't have become a father if he didn't understand children.

Curious about this disorderly den, and anxious to fill in the gaps in his fatherly knowledge, he ventured inside the next day when Holly and Charlotte were out in search of a brochure that featured sea cruises. His daughter had stopped just short of padlocking the door, and he could almost imagine a closed circuit camera recording his intrusion. Charlotte's devious brain, he had to admit, was beginning to daunt him.

Prowling guiltily round her crowded room, he found walls plastered with coloured pictures of her and her friends, love letters from some of them, and cuttings from newspapers, almost all of them about pop stars.

He went through the items on her dressing table in disbelief: Chanel N°5, nail polish remover, purifying gel for face and eyes, cleansing oil, self-tanning cream, Benetint ('the sexiest flush you can get'), lime and mint body milk, an invigorating oil for the body, and an array of brushes, all for the face. On the floor he saw a box of CDs, a baseball cap with an obscenity on the front, a bottle of Coca-Cola, and copies of *Heat* magazine.

He opened a drawer and found six bottles

of San Miguel beer, a small bottle of vodka and a half empty packet of cigarettes and a lighter. He didn't even know she smoked. Alongside the cigarettes were two sealed envelopes that he couldn't open without revealing that he had been there.

He crept out of the room and wondered whether he should brush the door handle for fingerprints. He was almost certain that twenty-five years ago, when he mixed with fifteen-year-old girls, they weren't a bit like this.

14

The long Christmas holiday, which now merged seamlessly into the New Year and even provided a hiatus in the busy life of Warren Goldberg, had meant that Andy's play had laid in a literary limbo for two weeks. But now the world was back at work and dormant dreams were revived in the frenzied offices of literary agents. Goldberg rang.

His call to the rented house which Andy had hastily vacated went unanswered, but making one final visit to the place to collect the post, Andy discovered the call when he dialled 1471. He was about to cancel the phone, too, and arrange for one to be installed at 3 Meadow Way, but first he rang Warren Goldberg Ltd with some apprehension. He had put a lot of work into the play, and one phone call could tell him that it was a wasted effort.

Maureen, Warren's secretary and shield, came on the line with her customary zip.

'Mr Devlin! Warren's been trying to get hold of you.'

'I've moved,' said Andy. 'I'd better give you

my new address. I don't seem to have a phone yet.'

Warren's voice was warm enough to give Andy hope.

'Andy! I think lunch.'

'Lunch?'

'What day can you come to town?'

When he returned to his new home, Clare was putting up curtains in one of the bedrooms.

'I've got to go to London tomorrow,' he told her.

'Can you remember how to get there?'

'Warren's buying me lunch.'

'What did he think of the play?'

'He didn't say.'

The home-building exercise that Clare was now engaged on was a source of great satisfaction. The fact that nobody had lived in the house before gave her a scope denied her in their previous homes, which had often arrived with fitted carpets and cookers, preordained colour schemes and built-in bookcases. She dumped the job at the delicatessen and embraced the challenge.

Sitting on the train the following morning, Andy experienced a rising nervousness about how Warren had reacted to his play. The idea that it had been a foolish mistake to attempt something so ambitious was not far from his thoughts. The very best that he could imagine was that Warren had a list of suggestions for amendments and improvements. Scripts like his traditionally went through many drafts.

He took the tube to Holborn and headed for Red Lion Square, feeling like the country bumpkin who had come to town. Confined by poverty and circumstance to his little office, it was a long time since he had seen such crowds.

Warren Goldberg Ltd occupied the bottom floor of an eighteenth-century house in the square. You had to go down steps to reach its bright blue door. Maureen rose from a computer to greet him. She turned out to be a buxom girl of about twenty-five. On the phone she had sounded older.

'It's lovely to meet you, Mr Devlin,' she said. 'As I told you, I loved your novel.'

'Call me Andy,' he protested. 'Where's the man?'

'I'm here,' said Warren Goldberg, emerging from a second office. 'Andy! Great to see you again!'

There was much hand-shaking and slapping of backs. Fifteen years didn't seem to have touched Warren much. He hadn't lost any weight or grown any hair. He still seemed to bounce as if the balls of his feet were made from rubber.

As they walked to the Italian restaurant Warren had chosen in Holborn, he talked about the problems of his job, the changing markets and the constantly shifting staff in the firms he had to deal with. Warren clutched his heart as if some physical strain was involved here, but the sun shone. The papers said it was the warmest winter for years.

Installed in the corner of their tiny restaurant, the chatty host delivered a eulogy on Maureen, the treasure in his office who was more interested in books than book-keeping, and had been plucked from college because of her knowledge of literature. She might be only a secretary now, but she would certainly become a literary agent herself.

They seemed to be skirting round the subject of his play, and Andy was scared to bring it up. Pouring wine and eating steak, Warren was keen to boast about his latest discoveries. They included a topless model's story, transmuted by the alchemy of fiction into a 400-page shagfest; seven cook books from seven TV chefs, all with their own equally unhygienic methods of preparing food; a first novel by a Cornish convent girl on the joys of incest; a multi-generational epic, set in Motherwell and called *See You, Jimmy*, that spanned Scotland's resentful years from Culloden to devolution, complete with dialect; three cheery novels by young authors so far known only to the public as comedians but now, suddenly, littérateurs; a whimsical travel book in which a one-legged man transports himself on crutches from Karachi to Kuala Lumpur, looking for jokes; and a sex guide from a Catholic priest. All these books Warren had swiftly placed in the grateful arms of successful London publishers, most of whom had their bosses in New York.

It was only when they reached the crêpe suzette that he was ready to discuss the matter in hand: the demands of his tournedos Rossini had evidently been too distracting for serious conversation.

'The play,' he said, looking Andy in the eye. 'What made you think of it?'

Trying to remember, Andy picked up his wine glass and found it empty. Warren apologized and refilled it.

'I was reading a history of Elizabethan England to get my mind off other miseries and Raleigh's story sort of stuck in my head.'

'And what a story! Author, explorer, knight! The first potato, the first cigarette! Sex, imprisonment, beheading!' Warren shook his head in awe at the exuberance of it all, but still offered no opinion on the quality of the goods.

'So what do you think?' Andy eventually asked.

Warren picked up his own glass now. 'It's a fascinating play, but it would make a better movie. You can do things on film that you can't show on a stage. Ships, foreign parts, tobacco plants. The queen in her carriage. Raleigh and Bessy Throckmorton making love in a haystack. It's a story with many settings. Visually it's a treat.'

'But I didn't write all that,' Andy protested. Warren was racing ahead of him, and the concept of a film was difficult to see in his stage-bound script.

'Don't worry,' said Warren. 'They'd have fifty screenwriters kicking it around. It takes twenty people to write a half-hour sitcom these days.'

'And one man to write *King Lear*.'

Warren held up a cautionary finger. 'Don't get snotty, Andy. We'd be dealing with the crème de la crème.'

'A fat cheque would shut my teeth,' he promised. 'What are you going to do?'

'I've already done it. I couldn't get you on the phone.'

'Done what?'

'I've taken the liberty of sending your work

to America. One of our former colonies across the water. They've handled their independence rather well, I always think. Two copies are winging their way to a couple of film companies in California. The biggest and best film companies, as it happens. They'd spend sixty million on it. What would the National Theatre spend? Probably a hundredth of that.' He smiled across the table. 'How does that sound?'

'Unreal.'

'Start at the top. That's the motto at Warren Goldberg Ltd. We can always lower our sights if there's no response.'

'What are the chances?'

'Hard to tell, but it's just what Hollywood loves, and it would pack them in at the multiplex. Pity Victor Mature's no longer around. The big historical movie was right up his alley. I'm afraid the film business today is notoriously unpredictable. It's a gamble but I'm certain it's one we should take.'

Andy drank some wine. His glass was empty again.

'It would be wonderful,' he said as Warren emptied the bottle into Andy's glass. 'But it's hard to imagine.'

'A strange remark coming from somebody with your imagination. Cheer up, Andy! The best is yet to come!'

The agent raised his glass, which mysteriously was still full. Andy realized that he had drunk most of the wine on his own.

★ ★ ★

Coming downstairs from her work in the bedroom, Clare was surprised to find Brad standing in the kitchen.

'Oh, hallo, Brad,' she said.

'Hi,' he said. 'Where's Andy?'

'He's in London seeing his agent.'

'No matter,' said Brad, and sat down. 'How's it going?'

Clare stifled an impulse to ask him how he got in. The back door was unlocked and he had presumably walked in, but it struck her as odd.

'It's all work at the moment, but it's going to be wonderful,' she told him. 'Where's Olivia?'

'At yoga.'

'Cup of tea?'

'That'd be nice.'

She switched the kettle on. The circumstances in which they had arrived in this house, she decided, made it necessary for her to be hospitable, but she was mildly annoyed at the way Brad had marched in uninvited.

149

'What's he seeing his agent about?' Brad asked when the cup of tea had arrived.

'His play.'

'Ah yes. Walter Raleigh. Is it any good?'

'I thought so,' said Clare. 'But it's a heck of a good story, whoever wrote it.'

'Andy's a good writer when he wants to be. Did you ever read his novel?'

'Of course.'

'Bloody hilarious.' Brad drank his tea. 'Andy's a lucky man.'

'I'm not sure he's had much luck,' Clare said. 'In fact, over the years he's worked very hard and had very little of it.'

'I was thinking of his marriage and his beautiful dark-haired wife.'

'Ah well, *there* he was lucky,' she said with a little laugh.

'You're a very pretty lady, Clare.'

He was looking at her in a strange way, as if he meant more than he was saying, and she felt embarrassed. Brad, permanently one of the boys, had never, so far as she knew noticed her much before. She had been quite happy with that, but now, she realized, with time and energy to spare, he could rediscover an interest in women. The thought alarmed her.

'Olivia's a very pretty woman, Brad,' she said. 'She knocks spots off me.'

'I don't agree with you,' he said, suddenly standing up.

For a moment she thought that he was going to move towards her, but luckily Greg came in with one of his questions.

'Mummy, why did they find elephants in Africa, and elephants in India, but none in north or south America?'

Clare was delighted at the interruption, but still managed to wish that her son could occasionally ask her a question that she could answer.

'I've often wondered that myself, Greg,' she said. 'Get your coat. We've got to go out and get something for dinner.'

★　★　★

'Had he been drinking?' was Andy's first question when he returned, confused by talk of Hollywood, from London. Clare was serving up a salad, which was all he wanted after his metropolitan feast.

'I don't think so,' she said, 'but he had a strange expression as if I should understand what he was up to.'

The news was as unwelcome to Andy as it was mystifying. Brad, for all his flaws, had never shown much interest in women. Nobody knew what he did at home, but the rest of the time since Andy had known him had been split between building up his public relations concern and drinking with friends. The temptations of the flesh which had lured others to cheap hotels or bizarre assignations in the back of cars, *en route* to the divorce court, had been of no interest to him.

Still, a few weeks ago he would have said the same about Clive.

'He just walked in!' Clare said. 'Does he think he owns us?'

This, to Andy, was the most worrying aspect of all. Did Brad believe that handing over the house and money had given him privileges he didn't previously have? Did he feel in some way that he was part-owner of this house, and access should always be available?

'Do you think I should have a word with him?' he asked.

'It's up to you. He's your friend.'

Andy saw that the ball had been lobbed back into his court, but didn't know what to do with it. Any comments from him, so soon after moving in, would tarnish a wonderfully generous gesture and affect their friendship in a way he didn't want.

'I think what I'm going to have to do is ignore it,' he decided. 'But we'll keep a close eye on what happens next. For a start, you could keep the back door locked.'

'Fortress Devlin,' said Clare. 'It's a funny way to start in our new home.'

'Needs must,' said Andy. 'Where's Greg?'

'He ate earlier, and is actually reading a book he found among his Christmas presents.'

'Harry Potter. Well, it's a start.'

Clare had now joined him for a salad in the kitchen. The dining room wasn't furnished yet.

'Tell me about Warren,' she said.

Andy waved an arm vaguely. 'Oh, he's got some fanciful notion about the movies. He sees Raleigh as a film.'

Clare raised her eyebrows. 'That's wonderful! Why didn't you tell me when you came in?'

'The fact that Warren sees it as a film doesn't mean that anyone else will. Don't build your hopes up.'

'Well, I can see it as a film. There's too much going on for a stage. Andy, you could be a dollar-earner!'

But for him the excitement had waned. The hopes raised by Warren's positive reaction to his play had subsided with the cheering effects of the wine. There had been too many setbacks, too many disappointments.

'It's only your optimism that keeps me going,' he said.

15

A familiar face appeared at Brad's front door one afternoon. It was the man with the ponytail he had met in the wine bar.

'Oh, hallo,' said Brad. 'We met before.'

Away from licensed premises, the man did not have the same non-stop conversation. He looked almost surly.

'Yeah?' he said.

'In the wine bar. Don't you remember? You'd taught a parrot to shout 'wanker'.'

The man was evidently not interested in these memories from the past.

'I'm looking for Charlotte Preston,' he said.

'Wrong house. Next door.'

The man nodded, turned and went. Brad was disappointed. He was bored. With the slightest encouragement he would probably have invited the man — Jason Marr, that was his name — in for a drink.

A minute later Jason Marr knocked on the Prestons' front door. Clive, who had been looking at a brochure about the Rover he was going to buy, opened it. An unprepossessing man with a ponytail was staring at him from the doorstep.

'I'm looking for Charlotte Preston,' he said.

'I'll get her,' Clive answered instinctively, but as he went upstairs he thought that this man was rather old to be calling on his daughter.

Charlotte was in her bedroom listening to the latest of many new CDs. To Clive they all sounded strangely alike. She was lying on her bed when he opened the door after a discreet tap.

'There's a chap come to see you,' he told her.

'Who is he?'

Foolishly he hadn't asked. 'No idea,' he said.

'Well, can you find out who it is? I might not want to see him.' The request was almost regal, but he didn't want to argue with her. It was his mistake.

He went downstairs again. 'She wants to know who you are,' he told the man at the door.

'Jason Marr.'

The name had an electrifying effect on Charlotte, who jumped off the bed and pushed past Clive as he stood in the doorway. Curious, he followed her downstairs.

'I told you I'd call at your house if you didn't keep your word,' he heard Jason Marr say, but then Charlotte persuaded him to be quieter. She came in after a minute, rushed back upstairs, fetched something and went down again to Jason Marr, who left soon afterwards.

'Who was that?' Clive asked.

Charlotte looked uncharacteristically rattled.

'A friend,' she said, and disappeared upstairs.

★ ★ ★

Brad suggested football. He said it was years since they had played and they all needed the exercise. They were surprised to find that he had bought a new ball, which he insisted on christening with the first kick.

'The return of the awesome triumvirate,' he announced.

'I don't think we were that awesome,' said Clive, trotting after the ball. The exercise felt strange to him, but he had welcomed the opportunity to try it. He thought it was a way of holding back the years. In his younger days he had been a Jackie Charlton figure, guarding the midfield. His galloping, ungainly appearance at a crucial moment in a game had been surprisingly effective at repelling invaders and robbing them of the ball. There was no grace and not much speed, but he was a difficult man to pass.

This afternoon was a journey into the past. In an adjoining field, Brad had put down a jacket and a sweater as goalposts, and then stood between them, defying them to score. He had been a cumbersome goalkeeper who was surprisingly quick with the full-length dive that tipped the ball round the post. His speciality was injuring encroaching forwards. When a high ball dropped into the goalmouth, it was the hopeful striker who was discovered soon afterwards writhing in agony on the ground and shouting impassioned messages to the referee while Brad booted the ball upfield. Referees at that time were notoriously sympathetic to goalkeepers, who took their share of bruises, and usually suspected crumpled forwards of trying to fake their way to a penalty.

Today, as they tried to relive former glories, they were surprised at what the years had done to them. The ball was a yard quicker than it used to be and less amenable. The legs were less inclined to do what they were told. A sprint for a wayward ball required a recovery period.

'How am I looking?' Brad asked, giving his Gordon Banks impression between the piles of clothes.

'Pavarotti doing the high jump comes to mind,' Andy told him.

Andy had once fancied himself as a George Best figure, running at defenders, swerving and hitting. It was an illusion, he knew, but thinking himself into the role improved his game. He scored regularly, and was flattened even more often by burly full backs who were not going to be made to look foolish by his fancy footwork. He stopped playing after the seventh knee injury put him in hospital and he could still feel a twinge in the joint today.

But he enjoyed kicking the ball with the other leg this afternoon, and was getting into the spirit of this reminder of how things used to be when Greg appeared in the field and asked to join them. His son wasn't born when Andy played, but his attempts to show him what he had missed weren't very successful.

'Too slow, Dad,' Greg said, taking the ball and dribbling round the others at a speed that left them standing.

'Of course he's younger,' Brad said. 'At his age I could — '

'Don't tell us,' said Clive, 'because we won't believe you.'

They limped back across the field afterwards, feeling little-used muscles beginning to stiffen.

'You had a visit from Jason Marr,' Brad said to Clive.

'How did you know?'

'He came to my house first by mistake.'

'Who is he?'

'I don't know. I met him in the wine bar once and we had a chat.'

'What worries me is, why would he call on Charlotte?'

'I could have a guess,' said Brad, 'but it's only a guess.'

'I'm listening.'

'Drugs,' said Brad.

★ ★ ★

Andy wasn't entirely convinced that his brief return to football had done him any good, but it had one unexpected benefit: it produced a welcome idea. From three distinct elements of the afternoon — the football, Andy's knee and Greg's appearance — there came the plot for a story.

No longer confined to a small bedroom, but comfortably established in the downstairs study with a new desk and new word processor, he felt an obligation to write something, if only to justify the recent expenditure.

The idea that came to him in the inscrutable way that ideas did was for a short novel for boys, maybe 30,000 words. It would be called *Luke's Magic Knee*. The story was assembling itself in his head before he could find a pen.

Luke would be a boy of about fourteen whose two main pleasures in life are playing football and riding pillion on his father's motorbike. One day, during one of their rides, a deer vaults a hedge and blocks their road. The bike swerves, skids and crashes. Luke's father has many bruises but his wounds are superficial. Luke is hurled through the air, lands in the road and badly damages a knee. Weeks in hospital follow with several operations.

But when he comes out, fearful that his football career is over, he discovers a strange thing. Metal inserted in his knee joint has given it magical properties. When he kicks the ball it leaves the ground like a guided missile and travels at terrifying speed and with great accuracy. His running, tackling and heading haven't improved but, if given the ball, he can score from anywhere on the pitch. He becomes the school's star player, but is quickly poached by more important teams. He plays for the town; he is signed up by Manchester United. At fifteen he plays for England.

Andy switched on the word processor and started to type.

Coming over the brow of the hill on the back of his father's Honda 900 at nearly a hundred miles an hour, Luke Beckett wondered how fast his dad rode the bike when he was not on the back. The machine would do 160 miles an hour, and his father loved speed.

Andy paused in his work. A deer would have to appear in a moment but he didn't know much about them. How big were they, and what colour? He thought of the reindeer he had seen on Christmas cards. What was the difference between a deer and a reindeer?

He went over to one of the reference books now installed in a new bookcase in the corner of his study. A deer was a ruminant, hoofed mammal, he learned. It didn't seem very helpful. As he returned to his desk, Clare came in with a cup of tea and some biscuits.

'What are you doing?' she asked.

'I'm writing. That's what I do. I'm a writer.'

'Just as well. Greg says you're rubbish at football.'

'That's kind of him.'

'What are you writing about?'

'Football.'

'Are you better at writing about it than you are at playing it?'

'Let's hope so.'

She left the room with a smile, and he turned his attention to the tea and biscuits. What he really needed, he thought, was one of those cells that some writers built in their gardens where they could scribble without the fear of interruptions. He had created his own interruptions here, as he realized when his new phone rang on his desk.

'I forgot to tell you,' said Clive. 'All that football knocked it out of my head. I'm forty tomorrow and we're having a party. A little food and a lot of drink. Be there or be square.'

'You've discovered my weakness,' said Andy. 'I like food and drink.'

*   *   *

When Clive had replaced the phone he sat motionless, waiting patiently for Holly and Charlotte to go out. Now that they had money they could hardly bear to stay in. The world was full of shops with their glamorous offers and colourful trinkets and suddenly, magically, the glittering temptations were all within their reach.

From the moment that Brad had mentioned drugs Clive's mind had hovered between disbelief and despair, but then he

162

knew, humiliatingly, that he had been deluding himself. The cigarettes, the beer, the vodka and the little white envelopes had shouted a message at him that he was reluctant to receive, a truth he wanted to avoid. Now he waited until he had the house to himself. It was time to face up to things — even though he knew what the awful consequences would be.

Holly had bought a new car, a Range Rover in Charleston green. It was the vehicle she had always wanted and never thought she would get. Its arrival even pleased Charlotte who, while ostensibly spurning the values of everybody else, still managed to see the Range Rover as a social trophy.

Clive waited until they had driven off and then went up to his daughter's lair. It amazed him that so large a room could become crowded so quickly. There was a new television in here now, with a video recorder, a full-length mirror draped in red silk, and a tall bookcase that was packed with videos rather than books. More letters and notes had been taped to the wall and he paused to read some.

Every time I walk past you my lips are burning, baby. I have fancied you for a long time. I'm looking forward to the party so I can get keen with you. I like your figure and your style. Your lips are like roses.

Jamie

I think you are very fit and nice. I'm sorry they expelled me. I think we had something special.

Carl XXX

Jeff has told me about you and I hear your a fine looking chick. Good stuff. Perhaps we will meet when I come to England in August.

Ryan

The discovery that his daughter evoked such passion came as no surprise. She was a pretty girl. But where this passion would lead to provided fresh material for him to worry about. Would she concentrate on her forthcoming exams with this horde of sex-crazed oiks beating a path to her door? Every time I walk past you my lips are burning, baby.

He turned his back on the letters and went to the drawer. Two bottles of beer had gone and there were fewer cigarettes in the packet. He found the two envelopes, tucked away now at the back of the drawer, and tore them open.

The first, as he expected, contained cannabis. He felt it, smelt it and recognized it. He had seen it a few times over the years. For some people no social occasion was complete without it. Once he had been persuaded to try it, but it didn't do anything for him and he lost interest. Discovering that his daughter was using it at fifteen horrified him. He had another thought: he was funding a drugs habit.

The other envelope, he could feel, contained pills, and he emptied them into his hand. Most of them were blue but there were a few yellow and green ones among them. All had the head of a rabbit imprinted on one side. He had read about Ecstasy in a trade paper at work and knew what he was holding. The tablets were always printed with some logo, like the rabbit, to inspire brand loyalty among abusers, and because they were synthetically produced in unsupervised laboratories there was no way of telling what exactly was in them or how safe they were. He also knew that it was a class-A drug, up with cocaine and heroin, and had killed eighty users in Britain in the last five years.

Confused and sad, Clive walked slowly across the room, sat on Charlotte's bed and tried to imagine what was going on.

Perhaps he was too old to understand the demons that drove today's teenagers. He had nothing to compare them with but himself. At sixteen neither he nor his friends had shown much interest in alcohol. Nobody smoked. Drugs were the ill-advised choice of a tiny minority who were already turning their backs on convention. But today they were all at it — and not just beer, but vodka, not just cigarettes, but dope. It couldn't simply be a question of money and availability. Such things were available when Clive was sixteen and he had enough money to afford them. But the money went on coffee bars, pop records, cinemas and girls. It was great fun at the time but it would obviously sound prissy today.

For a moment he had to ask himself whether he was failing to keep up, a cultural dinosaur stranded in the past, quite incapable of appreciating the way that things had moved on. Fashions changed, tastes changed, habits changed, social mores changed, even language changed. Had he pitched his tent in the past and now found that he was alone?

He stood up, put the drugs in his pocket and left the room.

* ★ ★

It was twenty-four hours before he could corner her. At first he had waited to see whether she would approach him about the missing goods. When she didn't, he looked for her. He wanted to get her alone so that Holly couldn't hear the conversation, which he was confident would feature Sandra. But Charlotte was going to a party — arranged no doubt so that she could avoid his own — and was preoccupied with ironing and allowing her mother to do her hair.

He finally found her in her room in the late afternoon. She was doing her nails. She looked up but didn't speak. He shut the door behind him and sat on her bed.

'I found something in your drawer,' he said.

She didn't bother to look up. 'I know you did. What the hell were you doing sneaking around in my room?'

'It's my house, too.'

'And this is my room. Aren't I entitled to my privacy?'

She was artful as well as articulate, and she had put him on the back foot before he had begun. By the time she had finished he would probably look like the guilty party.

'I'm your father, for God's sake,' he said.

'Don't remind me.'

'Don't try to be unpleasant, Charlotte. You already are.'

'If you didn't want me, why did you have me?'

'I didn't know it was going to be you, did I?'

This was becoming ridiculous. She had knocked him off course already.

'Well, now you've got me and I want my stuff back.'

'Your stuff?'

'It cost a lot of money.'

'That's another thing. Your pocket money in future will be three pounds a week.'

'Three pounds?'

'It's more than enough for the things you need. If it isn't, your mother will buy them. Anyway, what stuff are we talking about?'

'You should know. You stole it.'

He absorbed her implacable hatred. Earlier that day, to mark his fortieth birthday, she had given him a tie knowing quite well that he no longer wore them.

'And it's yours, is it? I thought you were going to pretend that you were looking after it for somebody else.'

'I can't *believe* that you'd open my private drawers. How dare you.'

He watched her nail painting. The nails were green.

'Strange as it may seem, I was trying to protect you.'

She looked across at him. 'I'm sixteen, for Christ's sake. At least I will be in a minute.' Her birthday was still a month away.

'You don't know everything when you're sixteen, Charlotte. You just think you do. Do you realize the dangers of these drugs?'

'What do you know about it? You're the last person to talk on the subject. Everybody smokes pot except you.'

'Ecstasy kills people. Do you know that much?'

'Only bad tablets. Mine are all right. I've taken dozens of them.'

'Dozens of them?' he repeated with surprise. She needed help. He could see that now. He was pretty sure there were clinics that dealt with that sort of thing. The difficulty would be in getting her to accept advice. 'And do they all use this stuff at school?'

'A lot of them, yes,' she said, and he thought of his conversation with the head-master, who had seemed helpless before a wave of teenage lawlessness.

'Well, it's going to stop,' he told her, 'and you can throw the cigarettes away, too. You can't afford them now.'

The brush had been put down and she was giving him all her attention. 'Brill! You're going to stop me! Why don't you end war and abolish poverty while you're about it?'

He stood up, feeling rather foolish. He could cut her pocket money and confiscate the drugs, but how could he control her when she wasn't here? He couldn't be at her side for twenty-four hours a day, and she knew it.

'I'm really tired of your cheek, Charlotte,' he said. 'God knows where you picked it up.'

He headed for the door, but she threw him a final question.

'Seen Sandra lately?'

He ignored her.

'I want my stuff back, Dad. I want my blue bunnies. Otherwise I'm talking to Mum.'

'Do what you like, Charlotte,' he said. 'You usually do.'

16

Four hours later, when some seismic mental adjustments had been made to transform him from humbled father to self-assured host, Clive was pouring gins the size of birdbaths for his guests and trying to exhibit the correct demeanour for a celebratory occasion. He was finding the transition difficult because it wasn't a milestone he welcomed. He told himself that forty years sounded a long time, but if you called it 480 months it didn't seem so bad.

There were other painful factors that impinged on his duty to smile. Although he now had money and a new house, and was going to treat himself to a Rover for his birthday, the joy this should create was tarnished by the ambivalent attitude of his wife and the dismal performance of his daughter. The only bright spot in the whole shebang was that Charlotte had left for her party before she had time for the talk she threatened with her mother.

There were just the six of them in the room. Clive had intended to widen the circle, but Holly had stamped on that idea. She foresaw a horde of unknown guests dropping their cigarette ash on her new carpets, desecrating her new bathrooms and drunkenly breaking glasses as the evening wore on.

When she went to the kitchen to prepare dinner, Olivia and Clare, in a gesture of sisterly support, followed her.

Andy stood by the fire, which blazed merrily despite underfloor heating and a surge in the January temperature outside. He was curious about how the Prestons had furnished this room, which was of course identical in size and shape to his own. His guess was that they had spent more money. The deep green carpet was thicker, the ornate furniture seemed more expensive. Over the fireplace an original oil painting of the Swiss Alps, chosen by Holly in preference to the sunny Spanish sierra favoured by Clive, had an elaborate gold frame.

He turned to the others, who were settled on the new sofa, confident that the work was being done elsewhere, and tried to pull his thoughts away from Luke's magic knee. That was the trouble with writing — it never entirely left you.

'What I can't understand,' he said, 'is why am I the only bugger who is still working?'

'You love it,' said Brad. 'You've been sitting at your desk playing with your dangling participles ever since I've known you. Pushing the mind to its limits! What's it like?'

'It's like trying to bottle smoke.'

'What are you writing, Andy?' Clive asked.

'A novel for boys about football. Half the length of an adult novel — about 30,000 words.'

'If a picture's worth a thousand words, I'd sooner take thirty snaps,' said Brad. 'I don't know how you do it.'

'You have to nurture the cerebellum, if you'll forgive the sesquipedalian usage.'

'You can tell he's a writer, can't you?' said Clive. 'What happened to the play?'

'Who knows?' said Andy.

In the kitchen, Holly was grilling fillet steaks.

'What's the vegetarian option?' asked Olivia. 'Champagne truffles? Scrambled duck eggs and caviar blinis?'

'Neither of those, Olivia,' said Holly. 'Mushroom stroganoff with coriander rice. Are you a vegetarian?'

'I am now,' said Olivia. 'I'm into everything. The seaweed diet, the apple diet, clay therapy, hydrotherapy, vinegar baths.'

'You look well on it.'

Olivia was wearing an ankle-length yellow dress with cinch belt, which seemed a little too much for the other women. Her short brown hair, stylishly cut back, had obviously been in the hands of a hairdresser in the recent past.

'Did you know that mosquitos don't bite vegetarians?' she asked. She made it sound as if this removed her some distance from the hoi polloi.

'I read something about this the other day,' said Clare. 'Oh yes, all the animals we eat are vegetarians, except for pike.'

'Anyway,' said Olivia, who wanted to move on. She smiled at them both in a dazzling display of white upper teeth. 'How are you two getting on with the Rowe munificence?'

There was an embarrassed silence as Holly and Clare each hoped the other would answer. Neither knew quite what to say. Both thought the question was tactless and shouldn't have been asked. Was Olivia looking for a grovelling display of gratitude, or was this an exercise in superiority?

'We're getting on fine,' Holly said finally. 'Will one of you open some wine?'

When they had finished their meal — rounded off with passion fruit jelly and ice cream — and drunk far more wine than usual, Andy said protocol dictated that Clive, the hesitant figure at the centre of this evening, deliver a few words about the anniversary he had unwillingly reached.

'I didn't like making speeches when I had to at work,' he protested.

'Nor did I,' said Brad. 'Making speeches is like pissing down your leg. It seems hot to you but not to anybody else.'

'Nevertheless,' said Andy, 'the guests demand it.' He banged his plate for a silence he already had, and Clive reluctantly stood up. His long frame bent over the table, and under the light the grey parts of his thinning hair seemed to have spread.

'A long time ago,' he said, 'about the time that the mammals took over from the dinosaurs, I was told that life began at forty. It seemed unlikely to me then, and seems even more unlikely now. My wife has discovered my inadequacies, my daughter hates my guts, and a career that should be soaring has crashed in flames. To cap it all, I discovered yesterday that such talent as I possessed at football has vanished with the years. So what is this life that begins at forty? And what lessons serve us in the future?'

Clive paused and looked round the table, but nobody had suggestions. Holly was watching him nervously, unsure what he might say after the drinks he had had.

'I'll tell you what I've learned, after twenty years of hard work and service to others. Life is bloody short, and you might as well

175

concentrate on enjoying yourself because nobody is going to admire you for your sacrifices and self-restraint. At forty your life is probably deep into the second half, as we ex-footballers say, and you suddenly discover, much to your surprise, that every year is quicker than the last. The song says it all: Enjoy yourself, it's later than you think. Cheers!'

He raised his glass and took a huge swig of the red wine it contained.

'A very moving oration,' said Andy.

'Thank you,' said Clive. 'I'm going to put some music on now. You may dance if you wish.'

'He sounded a bit pissed off,' said Brad as they filed back into the large sitting room.

'He's got all the cards, but not in the right order,' said Holly. 'Is it the male menopause?'

Clive had found a Barbra Streisand CD and her music soon filled the room. He then headed for the kitchen to fetch more wine. By the time he got back his wife was dancing with Brad.

'You're a very beautiful woman, Holly,' Brad whispered. 'Gentlemen prefer blondes.'

'Are you telling me you're a gentleman, Brad?' Holly asked. She saw this mild flirtation as double revenge — against Clive for his selfish little speech, and Olivia for her insufferable air of superiority.

'Yes, but I get the odd hormonal pang,' Brad was saying. 'Do you know that marriage is at its most unpopular for seventy years?'

'Particularly among those who are married,' said Holly. 'Do you find me attractive, Brad? Somebody has to. I'm sick of being Mrs Boring.'

'I'd have to be missing a few chromosomes not to find you attractive.'

'Really?'

'I always tell the truth when I'm drunk. In vino vomitas.'

'Veritas.'

'That's the word. Why don't you come round tomorrow and bring your body with you?'

'And Olivia?'

'She'll be at her kung fu.'

'Feng shui.'

'That's the word.'

'I think not, Brad,' said Holly, looking round to see where Olivia was. Responding to the wine that had been dispensed more generously than at her usual soirées, she was singing quietly to the music while sitting on the sofa with her eyes shut.

Andy was dancing with Clare.

'It's a long time since you danced with me, sir,' she said.

'It must be that football. It's reintroduced me to the physical.'

'Well, yippee,' said Clare. 'What do you think of Olivia's dress?'

'She's just naturally extravagant. Apparently she boils two pints of water when she wants a cup of tea.'

Clive came over.

'Is this an excuse me?' he asked. 'I used to dance.'

'Enjoy yourself. It's later than you think,' said Andy. He went across to Brad, who was working his way through the CD collection. The wine had made him nostalgic.

'Where's the Rolling Stones?' he asked. 'I used to get off to that stuff. Do you remember Venetia from Esher?'

'It was Ginna from Pinner, actually.'

'That's the girl. I knew it rhymed.'

The phone rang suddenly, a wailing call from the hall which rose above the music. Holly, who was refilling her glass, glanced at Clive dancing with Clare and decided to answer it herself.

Brad put his hand on Andy's shoulder. 'If sex had been invented this year they'd have banned it by now. You'd be in court for obscene behaviour. It's only tolerated because it's been sanctified by time.'

'What brought that thought on?'

'Wine,' said Brad. 'Wine and Mrs Preston. My pivotal monograph on the subject will follow shortly.'

'You've got a good title already. Wine and Mrs Preston. It sounds like Muriel Spark.'

Holly called from the hall: 'Clive!'

He left the room quickly and Andy reclaimed his role as Clare's dancing partner.

'How is our host?' he asked.

'This forty thing's really hit him, hasn't it? He talks as if he's been given six months to live, and is going to make the most of it.'

'It's the view through a wine bottle,' said Andy, as Clive rushed back into the room looking pale.

'It's Charlotte,' he said. 'She's in hospital, unconscious. They think she's taken an Ecstasy tablet. We're going to have to wrap this party up, I'm afraid.'

★ ★ ★

As Holly drove him to hospital in her new car, Clive was hit by a terrible thought: Had Charlotte been driven to a bad Ecstasy tablet because he had taken her safe ones? His second thought, that Holly shouldn't be driving after the wine she had drunk, was quickly dismissed. The shock of the phone call seemed to have rendered her stone cold sober.

Her headlights picked out the hospital's name and she ignored the car park signs and drove as near to the main entrance as she could. They fell out of the vehicle and rushed in through rain that had started during their journey. When they gave their name at the reception desk the girl picked up a phone, and soon a black nurse in immaculate white appeared from one of the long corridors that led away from the reception area.

'Follow me, please,' she said.

'How is she?' Holly asked.

'She is unconscious.'

No further information was forthcoming, and they followed the nurse in silence along corridors that bent and changed. The hospital had been enlarged more than once over the years and the old was now welded to the new.

Finally, in a small ward of eight beds, they saw Charlotte. She was lying, eyes shut, on her back, her fair hair sprawled over a grey pillow, and her hands, with their green nails, palms down on the outside of the covers.

There was a tube up her nose.

'My God,' said Holly, and started to cry.

'I'm afraid there is nothing you can do at the moment,' the nurse said, and Clive sensed that there was disapproval here, disapproval of stupid kids wasting valuable hospital time.

'I can sit with her,' said Holly, pulling a chair to the side of the bed. 'How long has she been like this?'

'She was unconscious when she arrived an hour ago,' the nurse said. 'A young man brought her in.'

Clive stared at his daughter, urging her to wake up, but there was no movement at all. He was thinking that the last time he and Holly had come out to see Charlotte she was lying on the floor drunk and being sick. Other parents, he imagined, went to watch their daughters in plays or winning races or playing the piano. Whose fault was Charlotte's sad story? Looking at her lying unconscious in the hospital bed, it was harder to blame her and easier to blame himself.

But he didn't know where he had gone wrong.

A man appeared behind them wearing the white coat of a doctor.

'Mr and Mrs Preston?' he said. 'Shall we have a word in my office?'

He was a short plump man with a round plump face and a rather large brown moustache. They followed him back down the corridor and into the room that was evidently his office.

'I'm Doctor Tupper,' he said, shaking

hands. 'Please sit down.' He waved them to two chairs in front of his desk, and then went round the desk to sit down himself. It was Clive's hope now that he wouldn't guess that he and Holly had been drinking. How dissolute could one family be?

'Do you know anything about Ecstasy?' he asked.

Holly, too tearful to speak, shook her head.

'Your daughter was at a rave — in a warehouse, I believe. Techno music, laser lights, frenetic beat, all that stuff.'

'She said she was going to a party,' said Clive.

'Well, these days, I suppose, a rave is a party, and Ecstasy is the club drug. I need to tell you about it. What it does is stimulate the central nervous system. The raver gets enhanced sensory perception, or importantly, the energy to dance all night. They reckon that about 300,000 youngsters take it every week.'

'So why is Charlotte in hospital?' Clive asked.

'That's where some end up, I'm afraid. It isn't the drug that poisons you. The deaths it has caused are what you might call extra-curricular, and they fall into three categories.'

The word deaths provoked fresh sobs from

Holly, and Doctor Tupper paused.

'I hope your daughter is going to be all right, Mrs Preston. We won't know until later.'

'She doesn't *look* all right,' Holly cried.

'She's in a coma,' the doctor said soothingly, as if this was a good thing. 'We're waiting for her to come out of it.'

Clive, overwhelmed by a feeling of helplessness, patted his wife's arm. 'You were saying,' he said to the doctor. 'Three categories?'

Doctor Tupper turned his attention with some relief from the weeping mother to the frowning father. 'The first is heatstroke, and most deaths fall into this category,' he said. 'What happens is the tablet in a hot environment increases body temperature, and vigorous dancing in a humid and over-crowded room can raise the body temperature to dangerous levels — over forty. What you get then are low blood pressure, accelerated heart rate, dilated pupils, and then convulsions. Death is caused by respiratory collapse. The second category is straightforward heart failure. The blood pressure and heart rate thing which Ecstasy causes can normally be handled by a fit young person, and those who have died have usually had an undiagnosed heart condition.'

Doctor Tupper picked up a pen, perhaps to help him concentrate, and looked at Clive. 'I think Charlotte is in the third category. Water.'

'Water?' said Clive.

'There have been at least three recorded deaths from excess water intake. The problem is that the drug has dehydrating qualities and if you're dancing flat out as well you need to drink about a pint of water an hour. But if you aren't dancing a lot, too much water is dangerous despite the fact that the tablet has made you thirsty. The drug appears to affect the workings of the kidneys, and water is retained in the body, especially in the brain cells which are water-absorbent. Eventually the pressure shuts down primary bodily functions such as breathing and heartbeat. Dizziness follows and then collapse and coma. That's where Charlotte is, I believe.'

'What's going to happen?' Holly was brave enough to ask.

'We're fighting for her, Mrs Preston. The good news is that a number of young people have been admitted to hospital in this condition and survived.'

'And it's water, not alcohol?' Clive asked.

'They're advised against drinking alcohol, I believe,' said Doctor Tupper. 'Alcohol only adds to the dehydration problem.'

He stood up. There were other patients.

'Get her off them,' he said. 'Ecstasy puts a tremendous strain on the heart, liver and kidneys, and habitual users can suffer long-term neurological damage.'

'Thank you, doctor,' said Holly. What she was grateful about was the suggestion that Charlotte would be around to receive this advice.

They were ushered out of the office and walked back to the ward on their own. The nurse was by Charlotte's bed.

'What's happened?' Holly asked, her face contorted by fear.

'Nothing,' the nurse said. 'I'm just monitoring her progress.'

'Is there any? Progress?' Clive asked.

'Not yet,' said the nurse. She made some notes in her pad and took them away, clipped to her belt, to a higher authority.

Clive looked round at the other beds. Half of them were empty, which wasn't the story he was getting in his newspaper. The others were occupied by young women. Usually you could tell what sort of ward you were in — young men with broken legs, women with babies, old folk looking glum. But there was no clue about the young women sleeping in here. He assumed they were recuperating from some operation.

'What are we going to do?' he asked.

'Well, we're not leaving,' Holly said, taking the chair. 'I'm staying here until she opens her eyes.' She leaned forward and looked at her sleeping daughter. 'Come on, darling. Wake up,' she said.

Clive found himself a chair from the other end of the ward.

'I think I'll try to find a coffee machine,' he said, placing the chair by the side of the bed but not sitting on it. 'If I'd known I was going to be up all night, I wouldn't have drunk all that wine.'

Holly turned briefly from her daughter to fire him a disapproving glance. 'I don't think your problems count much at the moment,' she said. She looked back at her daughter and slowly shook her head. 'I can't believe this child was stupid enough to take Ecstasy. Can you?'

'Three hundred thousand take it every week according to Doctor Tupper.'

'But Charlotte's got *brains*.'

'Where drugs are concerned, brains don't come into it.'

He sat down after all. He felt rather sick and couldn't face the quality of coffee that might emerge from a machine. Holly certainly didn't look as if she wanted one. Her face was gaunt. She took her daughter's hand and gave it a squeeze, but there was no response. They sat in silence staring hopelessly at the bed.

★　★　★

Summarily evicted from a party that he was enjoying, Brad sought consolation in the glossy pages of some holiday brochures that Olivia had collected on one of her shopping forays. He took this delivery as a hint that his wife had foreign travel on her mind, and he read the brochures carefully so that their destination would be one that he would enjoy too.

In a signal that they had both drunk enough, Olivia was making coffee in the kitchen. By the time she brought it in, he had made the decision for both of them.

'Listen, I've found this hotel on a white coral beach in Mauritius,' he told her. 'The turquoise waters of the Indian Ocean! De luxe rooms with balconies! It sounds like me.'

Olivia sat in an armchair and faced him. 'As a favour, I'll come with you. In the meantime I've had a thought.'

Brad was prepared to bet every penny he had in Coutts that this thought would end with his writing a cheque. 'Go on,' he said.

'Mummy and Daddy.'

Olivia's parents, now in their seventies, lived in a stone cottage in Lincolnshire and visited them only rarely. Her father, a retired railwayman, used to talk about coming to see the grandchildren but none arrived. Today he seemed to spend most of his time driving in his old Ford Fiesta to the bowls club.

'What about them?' Brad asked.

'We haven't given them anything yet.'

'That's true,' he said, feeling slightly guilty.

'And then there's Muriel.'

Muriel was Olivia's younger sister, married with four children, who lived in Lancashire where her taxi-driving husband was brought up.

'Muriel,' Brad repeated. Even sitting at home with the shops closed and locked, his wife could still devise ways to eviscerate the family fortune.

'It must be a struggle with four children. What does a taxi driver earn?'

'I've no idea. How much do you suggest we give them?'

'I thought half a million each would be about right.'

This was rather more than the amount Brad was thinking about. What on earth would Olivia's parents do with half a million? They were set in their ways, they didn't want to travel, they were unlikely to want to change houses. A new vehicle to replace the Ford Fiesta was probably the limit of their ambitions. But it wasn't a request that he could refuse. As a judge would tell him if he ever ventured into such murky waters, half the money was Olivia's. However, he thought a little judicious opposition was called for.

'Do you think this is a good idea?' he asked. 'Half a million in the bank and your parents will probably start worrying themselves sick about interest rates.'

'They know what we won. How mean do we want to look?'

'Of course we should give them something, but half a million seems excessive.'

'Not given the size of our win. Anything less would look offensive.'

Brad pulled himself to his feet. He was too rich for this sort of niggardly argument.

'You write the letters. I'll write the cheques.'

He left his wife with a smile on her face and made his way to his new office, which was no longer a converted bedroom but a proper study. He enjoyed sitting in here. All traces of Bradley Rowe Images had been dumped in the move. Instead vivid posters — Ali, Manhattan, Van Gogh — adorned the walls. There was a CD player on his desk, a new bookcase, and a dartboard in the corner.

He found his Coutts cheque book in the desk's top drawer and filled in two for Olivia's family. Writing all those noughts was still a novelty. Idly, he flicked back through the stubs and felt a sudden wave of anxiety at the way he had been spending.

He took a sheet of paper from his desk and compiled a list.

Olivia	£1,000,000
Car	£280,000
Homes	£1,800,000
Andy & Clive	£1,000,000
Olivia's relatives	£1,000,000

Over five million pounds! Half the money had gone in a matter of weeks! And he had thought that buying a £600,000 house having won £11 million, was showing a wise and prudent nature! It would clearly be possible, if he continued to spend at this rate, to be broke by the end of the year.

Such advice as he had been given in the wake of his win had been to invest the lot and live on the interest, but two things had dissuaded him from this course. One, he wanted to spend a lot of money immediately on houses and cars. Two, there was no one to whom he could leave an untouched lump sum of £11 million, which would still be intact at his death. Of course he intended to invest what was left after the spending, but the figures he had just been looking at suggested there might not be much to invest.

There would have to be a brake on spending (once the swimming pool had been installed), and a more economical approach to life must start now. He was imagining the reaction he would get from his wife when he explained the new dispensation to her, when the phone rang.

He picked it up quickly.

'Hallo?' Sitting at his desk and taking a phone call was an innocent pleasure now that work and stress weren't involved in the conversation.

A voice that he knew but couldn't quite place said, 'That you, Brad?'

'*Oui. C'est moi.*'

'You haven't gone all European on us, have you?'

'*Non.* Are you going to introduce yourself, or is this some sort of guessing game?'

'It's Jeremy.'

Of course he recognized the voice now. It wasn't one he wanted to hear. After the chilly night in Dorset, he would have been quite happy never to hear from Jeremy again. He was part of a guilty secret that ideally would fade into the past.

'Everything OK?' he asked. Jeremy could quite easily be the bearer of extremely bad news.

'Not everything, no,' said Jeremy, and Brad's mind raced ahead. A police helicopter had taken a photograph of the field, and the police, who were looking for a body, were curious about the recent digging. His imagination allowed the disaster to unfold. In the end, receiving no satisfactory answers, the police had dug up the field themselves and found the car.

'What do you mean?' he asked nervously. 'What isn't OK?'

'Life, the universe and everything,' said Jeremy. 'It's no scene being a farmer these days, Brad.'

'So I hear' Brad replied solemnly, relieved at Jeremy's evident unhappiness. 'They're top of the suicide league these days, aren't they?'

'It's not surprising. If foot and mouth didn't get you, the government will. They want farms to contribute to the tourism business, for God's sake. They want us to beautify the countryside. They're mucking around with the subsidies and think we're going to turn into gardeners. Of course, all they're doing is feathering their own nests.'

'It sounds bad.'

'It is bad. We're on a low anyway because the public wants cheap food. The supermarkets have got us by the balls. We can't win whichever way we turn. If I was starting again I wouldn't go within a hundred miles of a farm.'

'What are you going to do?'

'I want out, Brad.'

'Out?'

'I'm quitting the farm. I'm going to try something else. Engineering, maybe.'

'How are you going to do that?'

'Well, that's the point of this call, Brad. The word comes back through the family grapevine that you won over £11 million on the Lottery. I'm throwing myself on your mercy.'

'How do you mean, Jeremy?' asked Brad, not liking this unexpected turn in the conversation.

'I need a million, and you seemed the person to ask.'

An embarrassed silence was carried down the line to Dorset where Jeremy stood, eyebrows raised, in a frozen expression of hope.

'I can't do it, Jeremy,' Brad protested. 'I've had some heavy expenditure at this end.' He was looking at the list that he had just compiled of the cheques he had already written.

'Heavy expenditure?' said Jeremy suspiciously. 'I thought you won nearly twelve million?'

'I did,' said Brad, 'and half of it has already gone.'

The silence came from Jeremy's end of the line now.

'When you were desperate, I helped you instantly,' he said after a while.

And charged me a thousand pounds, thought Brad. But the reminder had sinister overtones. It wasn't blackmail, but there was a strong hint buried somewhere that this wasn't a request that Brad could refuse. He wondered whether the money was intended to be a loan or a gift, but he didn't ask because it would sound as if he could be talked into writing the cheque.

'I was very grateful to you,' he said. 'I think I paid you well. But a million pounds is another world, isn't it? As I told you, five million of my winnings have already gone. At this rate I'm going to be skint by Christmas.'

Another expensive silence was dutifully transmitted down the line. When Jeremy next spoke, the tone of his voice had changed.

'Is that a no?'

'I'm afraid it is. I've just written cheques

for a million for members of Olivia's family, and I've made a decision to stop.'

But in Dorset, quivering with fury, Jeremy had replaced the phone.

★ ★ ★

Clive wasn't sure whether he had fallen asleep. The chair was so uncomfortable that it couldn't have been for long. His wife was talking, he realized, so she could have woken him up without noticing that he had dropped off.

'I've always believed that these things are the parents' fault,' she was saying. 'If a kid turns into a thief or a killer, the parents have made a hash of the upbringing. Most kids aren't thieves or killers.'

It was a view that Clive had leant towards himself, but in the present situation it was a difficult one to accept.

'So where have we gone wrong?' he asked, as he struggled towards alertness. The pervasive hospital smell had left a taste in his mouth. A new theory, that exonerated parents, came to him quickly: once out of the house, youngsters were exposed to influences and beliefs that parents never heard about and so couldn't challenge or correct.

'Have we shown her enough affection?' Holly asked plaintively. 'When was the last time you hugged her?'

'That time she kneed me in the groin, I think.'

'I always thought that was an accident.'

Clive ignored this. 'She's had affection,' he said, resentful of the suggestion that she hadn't. 'She's had everything! But kids go out and want a bit of excitement. Life can be boring when you're young. We ask ourselves where we went wrong. I think it was in not vetting the company she keeps. With a completely different circle of friends this wouldn't have happened.'

'The royal kids smoked pot. What sort of circle of friends did you have in mind?'

'An intelligent one.'

He looked at the inert body of his daughter and was engulfed by a feeling that he had let her down.

At three o'clock the nurse reappeared. She had the harassed air of someone who had been allotted one job too many. She took Charlotte's pulse.

'It's good,' she said. 'She's strong. If she opens her eyes will you press that button on the wall?'

She hurried off, and Holly smiled for the first time since they left home.

'That's the most hopeful thing we've heard, isn't it?' she said.

'It's great,' said Clive with relief. 'Come on, Charlotte. Wake up.'

But there was no discernible change in her appearance, and they sat there for another hour, seeing their hopes rise and fall. The young women in the other beds slept as soundly as if they had taken Ecstasy too. Perhaps they were sedated.

Clive and Holly had passed through the tiredness threshold and were now stringently watchful for any signs of a change in their daughter's condition. Holly spoke to her frequently, hoping to stir some chord. She remembered reading about teenagers in comas who were roused by the songs of their pop heroes.

At four o'clock Clive moved his uncomfortable chair, making a scraping noise on the lino floor. Charlotte opened her eyes.

17

Strolling along the embankment with the polluted Thames beside him and a pale sun offering light but not heat above his tired head, Clive paradoxically experienced a cheerful feeling of release. The milestone of his birthday had focused his thoughts, and the long night in the hospital had left him curiously hopeful.

Charlotte was recovering. She would stay in hospital another day for observation and tests, but the doctors expected her to leave for home tomorrow.

On his way to the train, Clive had dropped in at the police station to acquaint them with the activities of Jason Marr. The police said that they had been watching him for some time, but lacked the evidence, as they put it in their language, to lift him. Clive insisted on his own avenging moment, and dictated a statement about Marr's visit to the Preston home, which had now disappeared into the voluminous police files.

And now he was going to visit the Stalag — as a free man. The grey-blue skyscraper where his old firm occupied the top two floors had imprisoned him for years. He had hated the stringent dress code, the rigorous time-keeping and even the anti-smoking jihad which had workers standing on outside balconies with their Silk Cuts like a clique of potential suicides. From his office on a clear day he could see Windsor Castle, but he was more concerned about the threat of fire or a terrorist attack. To prevent people plummeting to their deaths in hopeless leaps for safety, he had suggested that a supply of parachutes or hang gliders should be stored on the top floor, but everybody had jeered at his paranoia.

He had been asked to call in today by the finance manager to sort out the details of his pension. He had been paying in money for years and was entitled to something, but a career cruelly truncated by an errant bonk confused the accountants, who now needed his agreement and signature before arranging a new, reduced monthly payment.

The depression he had once felt at entering this building was delightfully absent. He took the lift to the thirty-sixth floor, thinking the job he once had was like a stone in the shoe. He didn't know as he emerged from the lift that in these lofty spaces he was now something of a legend.

'It's shagger Preston!' shouted Oliver from

advertising, alerting the others with his boisterous Essex humour. Soon they had deserted their desks to greet the fallen hero.

Rory, from the graphics department (who was a legend himself for cycling home after a vasectomy), came over looking depressed.

'How's life?' Clive asked.

'Long weeks and short weekends, as usual,' said Rory.

'You look as if you can't make up your mind whether to cut your throat or blow your brains out.'

'You're well out out if it, Clive. How did you manage it?'

'I think everybody knows how I managed it,' Clive said modestly. Secretly he found it reassuring to meet someone who was thoroughly depressed.

Barry, the dyspeptic head of cosmetics who commuted in from the Surrey hills where he lived in a house mysteriously large, came up to him and shook hands. With his tie-pins, cuff-links and waistcoats, he seemed trapped in the past; Clive had always wondered whether he wore sock suspenders.

'What are you doing these days?' he asked.

'Remarkably little,' Clive told him. 'I played football the other day. You should try it. You're not losing any weight.'

Barry, who had a penetrating mind but a

protruding belly, nodded sadly. 'One in six Britons are now clinically obese.' he said. 'I just read it in the house magazine.'

Dominic from pharmaceutics, who had a flat in the area with a rotating team of female companions, was anxious to say hello. Apart from a compulsion to tell terrible jokes, he had always seemed to Clive to be one of his more agreeable colleagues.

'You don't want your job back, I hope?' he asked.

'No thanks.'

'Good. You're an example to us all. Bonk and bunk, that's the formula. And then bank.'

'I'm on my way to accounts now,' said Clive. Before such envy he felt undeserving and hypocritical, but he wasn't about to reveal how strangely his life had developed.

He went off to meet the humourless gentlemen in accounts. It wasn't a place that he had often visited. The accounts department never quite belonged; they weren't involved or interested in the main thrust of the business. They were an ancillary outfit, like the people who worked in the canteen.

But the finance manager, a man called Street, was obviously familiar with, and fascinated by, the salacious circumstances that had led to Clive's premature departure from this booming organization, and he

201

talked to him as if he had been granted an interview with a currently fashionable Hollywood star whose sexual exploits had men everywhere looking at themselves nude in the mirror, despondently examining their deficiencies. Clive handled the heroic status that he was offered with suitable humility and left the room with a financial settlement that pleased him.

He walked back through the open-plan rooms, ignoring the cheery shouts urging him on to even more sensational sexual transgressions, in search of the lift. He was within a few yards of it when he saw Sandra. He had thought, when he entered the building, that he could avoid her. He knew the hours she worked, and where she would be, but as she approached him with a flirtatious smile he guessed that somebody had told her he was in.

'Mr Preston!' she said. 'Fancy finding you in here!'

'It's only a flying visit,' he said. 'How are you?'

'I'm fine.'

'And your daughter?'

'She's doing brilliantly.'

She was wearing denim overalls for work, but still managed to live up to the office nickname of Sexy Sandra. On his last two meetings with her, in the office and in the pub at home, he had been in a state of controlled panic but now, alone in a quiet recess on the top floor, he was pleased to see her. His little speech the previous evening about time running out came back to him as he studied her seductive eyes.

He said, 'Thanks for the Christmas card. I couldn't send you one because I don't have your address.'

'Well, let me give you it. You never know. One day . . . ' She put her hand deep into the pocket of her overalls and withdrew a purse. From the purse she produced a newly printed business card, which she handed to Clive. It said:

SANDRA DEACON
Lap dancer

Underneath was her address and phone number.

Clive stared at it unbelievingly.

'Lap dancer?' he asked.

'That's me,' she said with a nod and a smile. 'I told you I had two jobs.'

'And where,' he asked awkwardly, 'does this lap dancing take place?' The idea took some getting used to, but he could see that her firm, shapely body could easily be deployed in the professional business of male arousal. He found the thought of her gyrating sexily in public deeply erotic, and he hadn't even seen her gyrate.

'Clubs, mostly,' she said, and then added with glinting eyes, 'The money can be amazing. Some girls get £5,000 a month in tips.'

'With money like that you hardly need this job,' he suggested.

'The girls who make that sort of money dance every night. I don't get as much work as them. That's why I've had the cards printed. Anyway, dancing's in the evenings. Why waste the day when I can be earning money?'

Such industriousness was rare among the people Clive had encountered, who were apt to become scarce when the possibility of work was mooted.

'You're a good girl, Sandra,' he said sincerely.

Her face — the sexy eyes, the pert nose, the lipstickless lips — produced a huge smile at this accolade. 'I went back to that pub but you were never there,' she said accusingly.

'We moved,' he told her, 'but we've moved back now.'

'So you might be in there again?'

'I might be.'

He edged towards the lift with a small wave. He could imagine what obscenities would flow from his former colleagues if they found him here with her.

'Goodbye, Clive,' she said.

'Bye.'

He got into the lift and was halfway back to earth before he realized that she had used his first name.

* * *

Charlotte lay white-faced in her hospital bed and studied impassively the worried frown of her mother. Occasionally she shifted one of her legs as if it had been inactive too long. When she talked she spoke slowly as though speech was a talent she was trying to recall.

'When am I coming home?' she asked.

'Tomorrow, darling,' said Holly. 'They want you to rest today.'

'Where's Daddy?'

'He had to go to London.'

There was a silence. Holly found hospital visits painful, and this one more than most. The things she wanted to talk about — the Ecstasy tablet and why Charlotte used them — would have to wait. Her daughter was in no condition for an interrogation now.

'Has he gone to see Sandra?' Charlotte asked.

'Who?'

'His girlfriend.'

'I don't think Daddy has a girlfriend, dear.' It was a sign of how confused her daughter still was that she could come out with such nonsense.

'She's the office cleaner.'

Holly smiled understandingly at the prone figure in front of her. 'Is that what you dreamt?' she asked.

Charlotte betrayed some irritation at the question. 'Daddy screwed the office cleaner on his desk,' she announced slowly from her pillow. 'It's why he was sacked.'

Holly frowned. She was affronted more by the language than the message, which she knew to be absurd. What happened to the brain under the influence of Ecstasy?

'Don't use words like that, darling,' she said gently. 'It's not ladylike.'

'It's true, though,' said Charlotte, and closed her eyes.

Holly wondered whether she needed to sleep, and was prepared to wait there while she did. She looked a lot better than she had twelve hours earlier with the tube in her nose. All that was needed now was to get her home, feed her and keep an eye on her. The drugs

206

inquest would come later.

Charlotte opened her eyes suddenly. She had been thinking, not sleeping. 'Why don't you believe me, Mummy?' she asked.

There were several reasons that sprang to Holly's mind. One of them was that Charlotte had never been the world's most reliable witness. Facts were distorted, stories later shown to be untrue. But this wasn't the moment to go into that.

'Daddy was made redundant, darling. Don't you remember? You've been having a dream.'

'I didn't dream it, Mummy. I was going to tell you yesterday, but never got time.'

Holly was unsure how to proceed now. This was not the occasion for an argument with her daughter, who still looked fragile.

'And how do you know about it, dear?' she asked. 'Where did you get this silly story from?'

'Shirley Pickard.'

'Who's she?'

'A girl at school. Her father works at Dad's firm.'

Holly felt a flush of unease at this answer. She knew that a man called Pickard worked with Clive.

'And what did Shirley Pickard say?'

'That dad — ' She tried to find the right

verb ' — had sex with this Sandra woman on his desk.'

'She's lying, of course.'

'She's not lying, Mum. I talked to Daddy about it.'

Holly reeled back at this, and her tender expression disappeared. 'You've talked to your father about it? What did he say?'

'He said if I told you it would upset you.'

'He's right.' Her resistance to the truth was disintegrating, and it sunk in slowly like poison, breaching whatever protective membrane she had created in her brain. She stood up. She couldn't keep still. 'He's right,' she repeated. 'But are you?'

'Afraid so, Mum. Minging, isn't it?'

Holly put her hand to her forehead, struggling to believe what she had heard. There were several offences she could imagine her husband committing. Drunken driving was obviously at the top of the list, but she wouldn't have been surprised by some shifty practice at work in the cause of his business, or even a fist fight — he had enjoyed violent contact on the football field. But for him to be discovered in an adulterous sex act anywhere — let alone on an office desk — was outside the limits of her imagination. His appetite in that direction had never constituted a threat, and his faithfulness had never been in question. She was stunned. The disappointment and anger would come later.

Her intention to remain at Charlotte's bedside wavered now. Her head was full of other things.

'Do you mind if I go, darling?' she asked. 'You've given me a bit of a shock.'

'That's OK,' Charlotte said. 'I'm going to have a sleep.'

'Are you feeling all right?'

'Yeah, but I will come home tomorrow, won't I?'

'Tomorrow morning,' she promised.

★ ★ ★

Holly nearly killed a cyclist on the way home. It must have been her fault because he wore short trousers and a neat, white helmet so she presumed that he took his cycling seriously. She missed him by an inch. An angry driver is a dangerous driver, she told herself. At least the near-miss calmed her down.

But she still stormed into the house with her head full of revenge, and then, sitting in the kitchen, she found Brad.

'How on earth did you get in?' she asked.

'You left the back door unlocked so I thought I'd wait. You've been to see

Charlotte? How is she?'

'Pulling through, I'm glad to say. Where's Olivia?' It was strange for him to wander into her house uninvited, she thought, but she had too many other things on her mind to pursue it.

'I don't know. Yoga or sky-diving or mud-wrestling. Clive's in London, isn't he? So I thought I'd come round and see you.'

'Don't mention Clive. Do you know why he was sacked?'

'Yes. He shagged some tart on his desk.'

'So it's true.'

The humiliation wasn't helped by the discovery that everybody knew except her. She was so angry that she had to sit down.

'I can't believe it,' she said. 'What a bastard.'

Brad didn't say anything. He sat and waited for the anger to subside. He had nearly mentioned the Viagra but saw at the last minute that this might win Clive some sympathy, or even excuse his behaviour.

'What am I going to do?' she asked him.

'Drink this,' he said, and produced a bottle of cold Chablis from the floor. 'Got an opener?'

It was exactly what she wanted, she thought, as she got up to find the Screwpull.

The first glass disappeared with indelicate

haste: either the previous evening's wine or the long night in the hospital had left her dry.

Brad looked at her over his glass. 'A husband who's a problem. A daughter who's a problem. You deserve better, Holly.'

'I sure do,' she said, refilling her glass. 'What have I done to end up with these people?'

'Life isn't fair,' Brad agreed, watching her drink the wine. 'Especially for women.'

'What a change to talk to a man who understands,' Holly said. 'And I always thought you were an unreconstructed chauvinist.'

'Me? God forbid!' said Brad smoothly. 'I always believed women got the rough end of the deal.'

'And you're right. My God, you're right.'

'Have some more wine,' said Brad, pouring her a glass.

Holly decided to drink more slowly. She had missed lunch because of the hospital visit, and the wine was going to her head.

'What was it you said last night when we were dancing?' she asked.

'I said I found you attractive.'

'No, not that. Something else.'

Brad tried to remember his spiel of the previous evening.

'Well, I *did* say come round tomorrow, and

bring your body with you.'

'That's it,' said Holly, her glass already half empty. 'Why don't I?'

'Do you want to?'

'Revenge, Brad! Revenge!'

Brad stood up quickly, unable to believe his luck. The news of Clive's desktop copulation had reached Holly from somewhere at exactly the right moment for him. He took her hand.

'Let's go,' he said.

He led her through his back door so that nobody would see them. She stumbled across the sparkling kitchen.

'Oh, look! Olivia's got a Rayburn!'

'I know,' said Brad, not pausing in his drive towards the bedroom.

He chose one that had not yet been used, although it was beautifully furnished in preparation for the first guest, if there ever was one. Holly was taken by the 'shades of chestnut' colour scheme, but Brad was trying to remember the sequence of events that led to intercourse. Did he remove his shirt before he kissed her? In the end, relying on instinct, he found himself undoing buttons on the back of her black dress, which obligingly slipped off her shoulders and fell to the floor.

'I've wanted this for a long time,' he murmured.

Holly burped gaily. She had drunk the wine

212

too quickly. 'Let's do it, Brad!' she said. 'I'll show the bastard.' She removed her own polka-dot pants, and lay naked on a bright new duvet of many colours.

'This is bizarre,' she said, looking round the room, 'but a girl's gotta do what a girl's gotta do. I always wanted to sleep with a multi-millionaire.'

'Sleep's got nothing to do with it,' said Brad, pulling off his trousers and managing simultaneously to kiss his neighbour's stomach. There was a slim athleticism about her body that he hadn't expected. Beside her, he felt lazy, overweight and unattractive.

The feeling made him ask: 'You're all right about this, aren't you?'

'I'm up for it,' said Holly, 'but you don't seem to be.'

'All good things are worth waiting for. Or so my mother used to say.'

'My God, you didn't do it with your mother?' Holly asked, looking appalled.

'She was referring to something quite different,' Brad assured her, 'My erections were a secret.'

'This one's bloody invisible,' Holly said, reaching diffidently for the flaccid organ. Succumbing to her silken overtures, Brad was gratified to see an erection the size of a

Guinness bottle climb laboriously into view.

'Good God!' said Holly. 'Have you had an implant? I saw a picture like this once in a magazine when I was at school.'

'Black man, was he?'

'Donkey, actually.'

Her smooth hand, its task accomplished, fell on to the duvet.

'Don't let go,' Brad protested hoarsely.

'I don't want you ejaculating over my Rolex. I've got plans for this thing, Bradley Rowe.' She took hold of it again and put it where she wanted it. 'That's it, Brad. You've got the idea.'

* * *

When Holly went back to her house in a pleasantly flustered state she wanted food, a bath and a sleep, but instead found Clare on her doorstep.

'A social call on the Rowes?' Clare asked, surprised.

'Very social,' said Holly.

'Olivia's in London.'

'This is true,' said Holly. 'Brad, however, isn't.'

Clare could see where this conversation might lead, and chose not to pursue it.

'I came round to see how Charlotte is,' she

explained. 'I've been thinking about it all night.'

'Come in,' said Holly. 'Let's have a cup of tea.'

The tea arrived with a plate of small cakes and buns. Holly had eaten an Eccles cake, a brownie and a rum baba before Clare felt obliged to try one. They were sitting at the table in the kitchen, and Holly related the story of her night at the hospital.

'She's getting better all the time, and is coming home tomorrow, but thanks for coming round to ask.'

'What a nightmare,' said Clare. 'I wonder if I've got it all to come with Greg?'

'Clive, if you'll forgive my language, thinks it's all to do with the company they keep. So watch his choice of friends carefully.'

'Am I to gather that Clive's out of favour?'

'Do you know why he lost his job?'

'I do, as a matter of fact. Andy told me.'

Holly pursed her lips and shook her head. 'Everybody knew except me. What a fool I was.'

Clare didn't know what to say. But she knew enough not to take sides in other people's domestic disputes. She took a bite from the petit four she had taken from the plate.

'You seemed surprised,' Holly said, pausing

in her assault on the cakes, 'that I've been next door?'

'Well, let's just say that I wouldn't go myself. To tell you the truth I'm rather annoyed with both of them at the moment. Olivia's remark last night pissed me off, actually. It kind of put us in our place.'

'I quite agree with you. She always had a superior side, but now it's worse.'

'I know we must be grateful for their generosity, but what has it turned us into? Serfs? Do you know what happened the other day?'

'Tell me.'

'I came downstairs and Brad was standing in the kitchen. He'd just walked in, uninvited. Don't you find that spooky?'

'Was he after sex?'

'Luckily Greg interrupted us so I never found out. Do you think he was?'

'I'm sure of it.' Holly took a thoughtful sip from her tea. She had to tell someone. 'Do you know what I've just done, while we're on this subject?'

'Yes,' said Clare. 'You've been to bed with Brad.'

'How on earth did you know that?'

'You've just come from his house looking like a woman who has just been to bed with someone.'

Holly glanced in a mirror and laughed.

'I do, don't I? You see, he turned up in this kitchen, too. In fact he was sitting at this table waiting when I got back from the hospital.'

'It's outrageous, actually,' said Clare. 'I keep the door locked now. But why did you go to bed with him?'

'Three very good reasons. Revenge on my unfaithful husband, and revenge on the snooty Olivia who thinks she owns us.'

'That's two reasons.'

'He brought a bottle of very good wine with him and I drank most of it.'

'I'm not sure that adds up to one good reason for having sex with Brad Rowe,' Clare decided. The news amazed her: Holly wasn't that type of woman. She guessed that the principal factor had been the wine.

'I feel all the better for it,' Holly said cheerfully. 'I feel that I've squared the accounts.'

'So now you can forgive Clive?'

'I certainly can't,' said Holly vehemently. 'I've got a certain advantage. I know about him and the cleaning lady, but he doesn't know about me and Brad.' She smiled triumphantly at this summary of the situation. 'I must say,' she said, 'that Brad's got the most enormous — '

'Don't tell me, Holly,' said Clare, holding

up a hand. 'I don't think I'm strong enough today. I'd better get back. Andy has a very attractive girl next door and the way things are going round here he's probably bonking her on the dishwasher.'

18

A magazine whose garish façade was familiar on the shelves of supermarkets had commissioned a series of articles on people who were 'famous for fifteen minutes' — one-hit wonders from the world of pop music, injured sportsmen, vanished newsreaders, drug-crazed actors, disgraced politicians, forgotten heroes, and ladies, no longer young, who in their voluptuous heyday were briefly celebrated for disastrous liaisons with sex-starved princes or presidents. And among the dross caught in this inquisitive net, as it bumped along the bottom, was Andy Devlin, the author of one successful novel and unheard of since.

The reporter was called Gaby and she sat on a stool in his study displaying endless legs. She looked about nineteen, which meant that she was four when the novel was published.

'I read your book yesterday,' she said proudly, as if this was more than she could reasonably be expected to have done.

'Did it seem dated?'

'The prices seemed a bit odd. Where would you get a house today for twenty thousand?'

Andy hadn't thought of that.

Other things, he soon discovered, had changed since he last submitted to an interview. The interviewer then had been a shy young man with immaculate Pitman shorthand who diligently filled page after page of his reporter's pad with the stumbling effusions Andy offered him.

Gaby eschewed notebooks. (There were journalists today, Andy heard, who had never held pen or paper.) She thrust a small Matsui dictation machine to within a foot of Andy's mouth as he sat at his desk, and would later knock out her version of this meeting on an office computer as she listened to her machine through earphones.

'Raging Hormones,' said Gaby. 'Good title, but by today's standards the hormones didn't rage that much.' She regarded Andy much as an archaeologist might examine an old fossil. She had long, straight blonde hair that fell forward and covered her breasts as she leant towards him.

Andy looked back at her. His tale of promiscuous youth had seemed raunchy at the time, and it was difficult for him to accept that it would seem less so now. Sex was sex — or had they invented something new?

'You mean it isn't dirty enough?'

Gaby pushed her bottom lip forward as she

considered this. 'The language is pretty restrained,' she decided, 'and sometimes the characters are shocked by something that doesn't seem so very shocking today. For instance, when Stephanie and Danny do it standing up against the church door, I think you intended that to be scandalous, but today people would say, 'So what'?'

'That's progress,' said Andy.

'The jokes are good, though,' she said, as if she felt she had been too hard on him.

'Some of them have gone into the *Penguin Dictionary of Modern Quotations*,' he told her proudly. She ignored, or didn't hear, this, but he trusted her machine to pick it up.

'Tell me what you are doing now. You're married, I gather?'

He gave her — or her machine — a brief résumé of his life, the long conspicuous eclipse that was the reason for her visit, and he could see as he talked that she was confused.

'You say that you're still writing and not earning, and yet — ' she waved an arm round the room ' — all I see here are the trappings of success. A lovely house, and wasn't that a Lotus Esprit I spied in that large garage?'

For a moment he was thrown. Brad wouldn't appreciate the story of the houses appearing in a magazine, and Gaby, distracted from her mission, might think it a better story to write.

'That's how it is with books,' he said, wishing it were true. 'They continue to earn. George Orwell's widow made far more out of his work than he ever did. Scott Fitzgerald ended up as one of sixteen dialogue polishers on *Gone With the Wind*, but his descendants lived well on his royalties for years after he died.'

'Who?' said Gaby.

Suddenly she produced a camera from her bag. She was obviously a girl of multiple talents, and the old-fashioned photographer had gone the way of the printer, the pen and the notebook. He sat on his desk and produced for her a suitably melancholy expression. Whatever happened to Andy Devlin?

'What are you working on now?' she asked as she prepared to leave.

He told her about the play he had written.

'Much more your métier,' she said, and he could see that in the postmodern recesses of her mind he was a contemporary of Raleigh.

★　★　★

Clive arrived home in good humour. His day could not have gone better. Not only had the pension business been settled satisfactorily and a friendly relationship with Sandra been established; he had also stopped off on the way home to collect his new car.

The pale grey Rover, a picture of elegance, stood in his drive like a status symbol. He walked up to the house and opened the front door.

'Hey!' he called to Holly. 'Do you want to see my motor?' The new acquisition, he realized, had produced an almost boyish excitement, but no human voice came back to share it.

He went into the kitchen. His nose collected no hint of a dinner in preparation, and the room was empty. He walked back through the long house to the sitting room where Holly was relaxing in an armchair, reading *Vogue*. She was wearing what he always thought of as her Gorgon stare.

'I've got the car,' he told her.

'I heard you.'

'Aren't you interested?'

'Not remotely.'

'I see,' he said and sat down. He looked across at her for an explanation but the magazine was receiving all her attention. He could guess what had happened. Charlotte had recovered sufficiently to put in the poison. He sat there waiting, determined that she would have to speak next. It was some time before she did.

'And did you see Sandra today?' she asked, without lifting her eyes from the magazine.

'As a matter of fact I did. She works there.'

'And screws there. I've heard all about your disgusting behaviour.'

'Obviously. Charlotte is getting better, I gather.'

He sat back and waited for the onslaught. He had hoped that his daughter would keep her mouth shut after the trauma of her hospital experience. He thought she might emerge from it nicer and wiser, although as he sat on the sofa he couldn't think of any reason why this should be so.

'I want a divorce,' Holly said, putting down her magazine. The bleak announcement came as a shock to him. Even now, with his crime exposed, he hadn't thought things were as serious as this.

'Are you sure?' he asked.

'Oh, I'm sure. Do you think being married to you is fun?'

'We've had our moments.'

'Remind me. Do you think I enjoyed all those social functions I had to attend because of your job? God, what a bore that was. Having to listen to some lying reptile going on about your latest exciting product — a callus-removing cream or a cure for piles.'

'I wasn't exactly thrilled by that stuff either, but it provided you with money for the things that you wanted.'

'The things that I wanted? We'd go to Marbella when I wanted to visit Locarno, or Padstow when I preferred Torbay. We flew when I wanted to sail, and when I asked for a dog you bought a cat.' Her sullen expression lit up now with the satisfaction of an attack. 'And when you got home from work and I put your dinner in front of you, you ate it without even noticing what it was. It might have taken me half an hour, it might have taken me two hours — it didn't matter. Did you ever come home and ask what sort of day I'd had? You were too full of what sort of day you'd had.'

She paused, searching for more ammunition. Clive sat there, taken by surprise at how the Sandra incident had expanded into this. He remembered the list he had compiled, itemizing their different tastes, but he had never imagined that the fissures were so deep. If this ends in divorce, he vowed to himself, I shall never get married again.

'You weren't even consistent because you don't have any convictions,' Holly said now. 'You thought your daughter was the most wonderful person on earth, and now

225

apparently you think she's the worst. You had a socialist's distaste for the rich, but spent every waking minute trying to become it. You took a high moral stand on other people's adultery, and ended up bonking the cleaner.'

'I don't think Charlotte's the worst person on earth,' he protested. 'I love her. But there are things about her you should know, and would know if you kept a closer eye on her. In her room upstairs she had cannabis, Ecstasy tablets, vodka, beer, cigarettes and God knows what else. And she's only fifteen.'

Holly was shocked now. 'And you didn't *tell* me?'

'I confiscated the drugs. Which was why she told you about Sandra.'

'I see. If you told me about the drugs, she'd tell me about Sandra?'

'Something like that.'

This, to Holly, was the biggest crime of all. 'Good God! Well, we can see who the weak link is here, can't we? A girl of fifteen can bully you into silence because of your own disgraceful behaviour! You're more despicable than I thought.'

Clive stood up. There didn't seem to be anything else to say, or if there was he didn't want to hear it.

'You'll be moving out then?' he said.

Holly looked up at him from the armchair.

'Moving out? Why would I do that?'

'I believe that couples who get divorced don't normally go on living under the same roof.'

Holly's rage now was phosphorescent. 'Isn't that typical of you? I've got as much right to this house as you have. More. I've got a daughter to bring up. *You* move out. You broke the rules. You didn't even buy the place.'

He walked out of the room, white-faced, and went upstairs to have a shower. Then he put on more casual clothes than the suit he had felt obliged to wear to London, and rang Andy.

'He's not here, Clive,' said Clare. She sounded nervous. 'How are you?'

'Not that good, tell you the truth, Clare. Where's your man?'

'He picked up his new Lotus today and is driving around somewhere like an excited schoolboy. You can reach him on his mobile.'

★ ★ ★

Cruising through the darkened countryside in his new car, familiarizing himself with its instruments and discovering its breathtaking potential, Andy feared that a deer might jump a hedge in front of him, like the scene in the story he was writing. Sometimes it was hard to tell where fiction ended and reality began.

Reality extended every day, pushing into corners once occupied by the dreams and fantasies that might fill his head in bed. In a conversation with Clare, before he came out he had learned, to his utter stupefaction, that Holly had gone to bed with Brad, which was not something he could have imagined, no matter what fantasies were dancing in his brain. Holly had always struck him as a cool, even remote, figure, and Brad had never shown the lascivious yearnings for passing women that a lot of men were happy to talk about. Picturing them together in bed he found impossible.

'Are you sure she didn't make it up?' he had asked.

'Why on earth would she do that?' Clare replied.

'I don't know. To hurt Clive?'

'I don't think Clive is going to know about it.'

There was something else that worried Andy and he tried to remember what it was as he swooped down country lanes negotiating bends too quickly, testing the torque and the grip. He liked driving at night. If there was a car approaching you round the next bend you were warned by its lights.

He remembered what it was. Brad had

wandered into the Prestons' kitchen when there was nobody there, just as he had appeared in Clare's. He had never raised the matter with Brad, but now he wished he had. The two incidents damaged their relationship in some way and shifted it to a different level. In fact, when he thought about it, the balance of their friendship had changed imperceptibly ever since they moved. Perhaps it was inevitable. They no longer met Brad as equals, and there was no other way for a normal friendship to flourish.

As he turned on to an A road and put his foot down, he had to remind himself that it was also Brad's money that had paid for this car. He hit a hundred very quickly and eased off, alarmed at the power. How much nicer it would have been, he thought, if it had been his earnings that had enabled him to own such a vehicle. He had dropped down to sixty when his mobile phone on the front passenger seat started to bleep.

It was Clive. He sounded terrible.

'I'd like to talk,' he said. 'Where are you?'

'I'm in my new car. Hang on. Let me slow down a bit.'

'Could we meet in our old pub?'

'I'll be there in fifteen minutes,' Andy promised, 'although in this car it will probably be ten.'

19

Eddie, the occasionally cheerful landlord of the Hen and Chicken, brightened up when he saw not one but two new cars arrive in his gravel car park. He suspected, in his struggle towards financial independence, that a car park full of motorbikes and muddy Escorts carried the wrong message to the passing trade who hurried by in search of classier joints. When he saw who the drivers were his spirits were hoisted another notch.

'The drinkers return!' he said. 'The recession's over!'

The expression on Clive's face, however, did not suggest that he would be entering wholeheartedly into this little celebration, and even when Eddie, in a rarely seen moment of generosity, bought the first drinks, it was hard for him to respond with a smile.

He sat at the counter and looked at Andy. 'I've been snitched up,' he said.

'Snitched up?'

'All right. Grassed up. Charlotte's told Holly why I lost my job.'

'Why did she do that?'

'Because I confiscated some drugs I found

in her room. The vindictive little bitch. I was trying to save her life, for Christ's sake. Now Holly wants a divorce.'

'Is that what she said?' Andy asked, surprised.

'That and a lot of other things about me and my job being boring. Also, I'm unappreciative, uncommunicative and selfish. She's been going at me for the last hour. She's got all the words.'

'It sounds quite comprehensive. Why did she call you selfish? I always thought you were rather generous with your family.'

'Oh, I don't know. We went to Marbella when she wanted to go to Locarno. Christ, we've been to Locarno three times and sat and stared through the mist at that bloody lake.' He ran his fingers through his thinning hair and then, elbows on the bar, buried his face in his hands. Andy had never seen him like this and wondered how to deal with it. The Preston marriage had chugged along for years without any signs of dissension.

'She'll come round,' he suggested.

'No, she won't,' Clive said from behind his hands. 'And do you know what? She wants the house.'

'She wants you to move out?'

'That's her idea. She says she has as much right to it as I have, which of course is

231

correct. I'm going to end up with four different homes in four months.'

'Christ,' said Andy, 'are things really this bad?'

Clive removed his hands. 'I'm a pessimist. That way I'm never disappointed and occasionally I have a nice surprise. But I can't see any nice surprise here.'

Eddie was suddenly leaning over the counter. 'If ignorance is bliss, why aren't more people happy?' he asked.

'Very good, Eddie,' said Andy. 'Have a drink and get us some. We're going to put our faith in the restorative powers of your lager.' He was wrestling with a dilemma. Normally he kept clear of other people's marital wars. They always ended suddenly, leaving you looking foolish if you had taken sides. But the flak Clive was getting was unfair. The man was fighting with both hands tied behind his back.

'I've gone off hemlock,' he said. 'What about a shotgun to the palate?'

'If your IQ was ten points higher you'd be a plant.'

Clive picked up his new pint of lager while Andy handed Eddie money.

'You don't realize how serious it is,' he said when this transaction had been completed. 'Holly and I had always been faithful to each other. She's a stickler on the morality front.'

'Well, the mask slipped this afternoon,' Andy told him. 'Brad the Benefactor took her to bed.'

'How do you mean?'

'You know. Man. Woman. Bed. Oh, of course you don't know. Think desks, Clive.'

'You mean he — '

'Into a trance, apparently.'

Clive sat in silence, staring at his lap.

'How do you know this?' he asked quietly.

'Clare went round to see how Charlotte was, and Holly told her. She'd just got back from her social engagement in the Rowe bedroom. The interesting thing is how it started. Brad was waiting in your kitchen with a bottle of wine when Holly got back from the hospital.'

'In our kitchen?'

'It wasn't the first time that's happened. Clare came downstairs the other day and found him in *our* kitchen.'

Clive gave him a funny look. 'Didn't you do anything about it?'

'I didn't actually. He'd just bought us the house, and it didn't seem the moment to start complaining. I just told Clare to keep the back door locked.'

'You know what this is?' said Clive. 'It's *droit de seigneur*.'

'Don't give me that stuff, Clive. I'm still recovering from snitched up.'

'*Droit de seigneur*. The right of the feudal lord to copulate with the vassal's bride.' He squinted at Andy as he had another thought. 'Do you think he bought us these houses because he fancies our wives?'

'That's a very sinister idea.'

'Well, these are pretty sinister times. Holly and Brad? I can't believe it.' He drank some lager and then peered into the glass as if the truth was in there somewhere. 'I can't believe what's happened in the last twenty-four hours.'

'Do you wish you hadn't accepted the house?'

'I do now. We sold our souls for a pile of bricks.'

'There was also the money, though. Think of the two new cars in the car park outside!'

Clive shook his head. 'What a materialist you are, Andy. You sit here surrounded by human tragedy, and all you can talk about is money!'

'Well, it made a big difference to me. I've never had any. While I was staring at a blank sheet of paper and wondering where the words were going to come from, you were poncing off down to London and raking it in with your pricey placebos and dubious

234

unguents. I was in a supermarket not many weeks ago and when I got to the checkout I had to put several items back on the shelves because I didn't have enough money. Has anything so embarrassing ever happened to you?'

'Of course not. You were our token pauper. Everybody should know one.'

'Well, I got a bit sick of it, frankly. Clare's had to put up with an awful lot.'

'She'll have to put up with a lot more if she forgets to lock the door. And that's the bloody point. What's this great act of generosity costing us?'

'It's changed our relationship with Brad. I was thinking about it in the car.'

'Changed it? It's ended it. Do you think I can talk to him now?'

Andy could understand the anger, but was saddened that such a magnificent gesture was now tarnished by this squalid sequel. Clive's turbulent mind, however, had found other horrors to explore.

'I wonder whether it's happened before?' he said ruminatively. 'The idea that your wife's getting bonked brainless while you're struggling towards your first coronary doesn't cross your mind.'

'I shouldn't think so,' said Andy. 'She's not the type.'

'Well, she's the type now! Her Nastiness has shot herself in the foot this time. This changes everything.'

'You mean she's as guilty as you are?'

'Exactly. Why should I move out? At least I had the excuse of Viagra. It changes any divorce case, as well. She can hardly sue me for adultery when she's been at it herself. Who's the guilty party now?' Clive, plunged into a black mood by Andy's news, had now risen above it, glimpsing unexpected benefits from his wife's rendezvous with Brad. He seemed almost cheerful. 'I can go home with a clear conscience and crucify the slag.'

'I should ease up on the clear conscience bit,' Andy said. 'Remember St John?'

'I hate Liverpool. You know that.'

'I'm not talking about the footballer, you prannet. I'm talking about casting the first stone.'

'Holly has already cast the first stone, and she wasn't without sin when she did it. Now it's my turn.'

★   ★   ★

But Holly was deeply asleep when he got home. He crept into the bedroom, and then he crept out again. The idea of sleeping beside her made him uneasy. He could wake up in the morning minus a bit, and he knew which bit he would be minus.

He went into the next bedroom, already beautifully furnished by his wife in anticipation of a visit some day by her widowed mother, and fell into the new bed. Expecting a sleepless night racked by guilt and remorse, he was surprised to find when he woke up refreshed that it was ten o'clock in the morning. The explanation, he realized, was that neither he nor Holly had had more than four hours sleep the previous night.

He found her downstairs eating a bowl of cereal in the kitchen. She had only just got up herself. She didn't speak when he came in.

He made himself tea and toast and sat at the table opposite her.

'What a hypocritical bitch you are, Holly,' he said.

She looked up at him. 'Do we have to talk? It was very peaceful in here a moment ago.'

'You gave me the works about Sandra, and all the time you'd been to bed with Brad.' He watched her carefully for her reaction, but she was unmoved.

'Have you finally gone mad?' she asked.

'You can't bluff it, Holly. I know what happened.'

'If I were going to go to bed with somebody, which I'm not, you think I'd

237

choose Brad, do you? You didn't get a dose of syphilis from Sandra, by any chance? It can affect the brain.'

He was surprised at the pungent tone her conversation had developed. For years her carefully modulated speech had exuded sweet reasonableness, but now suddenly she had the caustic tongue of a whore. It was a talent she had managed to conceal from him, like a taste for adultery, and he wondered what else he had missed and how little he knew her. The decorous housewife had disappeared.

He said angrily, 'For Christ's sake, you loopy tart, everybody knows you went to bed with him. Clare knows, Andy knows, I know.'

She gave him a defiant glare.

'Even if I went to bed with Brad, which I don't for one moment admit, it would have been after your sordid bloody sex fling on a desk. So don't come all whiter-than-white at me.'

'The circumstances in which I had sex in the office were rather unusual,' he told her. 'I'd been given some Viagra. I was planning to come home and make love to you.'

'That would have made a bloody change after a day in the office. What was the problem? The old premature orgasm?'

He ate his toast. There must be a way to obtain the satisfaction of a confession, but his blows glanced off her, like those of a boxer facing an opponent whose face is smeared with Vaseline.

'Why don't we go and talk to Brad about it?' he suggested.

'You go and talk to Brad about it. He'll sort you out. In case you've forgotten, we have to fetch Charlotte this morning. Or perhaps you don't want to come? She'll expect to see you.'

'Of course I'll come,' he said, 'but there are a few things to clear up first. If we're going to talk about Sandra in a divorce court, we're going to talk about Brad, too. And now that I'm no longer the only guilty party round here, I feel no obligation to leave this house.'

This two-pronged assault appeared to have achieved something because Holly fell silent. He waited for the ball to come hurtling back, but she was occupied now in putting cups and plates into the dishwasher, and seemed to have lost interest in the verbal fray. He went upstairs to shave, wondering how all this was going to end. He didn't doubt that a certain amount of rethinking was going on downstairs, and a new offensive being planned. She was, he now knew, a formidable adversary. Behind that beguiling middle-class innocence there lurked a hard, malevolent streak which she had passed on intact to her daughter.

In fact Holly hadn't been thinking about

Clive at all. She had been worrying about Charlotte. When he came downstairs for the trip to hospital, she asked, 'Whose car are we going in?'

'Mine. Charlotte hasn't seen it.'

'Well, do you think we can put on a show for our daughter? The girl's been desperately ill.'

★   ★   ★

She was sitting on her bed waiting to be liberated. Her pale face broke into a smile when she saw them come in, and she stood up and gave them both a kiss.

'How are you, darling?' Holly asked, feeling her forehead.

'Yeah, I'm OK,' she said, ' 'cept that you can't get any sleep in this place.'

Clive didn't think that she looked OK, and wondered what damage had been done. They had a few words with the nurse and went out to the car park.

'You look rank in those jeans, Dad,' Charlotte remarked.

'But wait until you see the new car,' he told her.

She studied the shiny grey vehicle appreciatively and pronounced, 'Wow!'

If she detected friction in the car, she

didn't reveal it. She talked about the girl in the next bed to her who had survived a potentially lethal cocktail of heroin, vodka and barbiturates. 'Two young men kill themselves every day in Britain,' she told them. 'Weird or what?'

'Did you learn anything else in hospital?' Clive asked hopefully.

'Yeah, I learned that most people aren't enjoying themselves. They're just passing the time.'

This wasn't the reply he was seeking, and he drove on in silence before parking his car neatly in the drive. Winter had resolutely refused to appear and a spring-like sun would soon be inducing early blossoms.

When they went indoors Charlotte made straight for her room to be reunited with the joys of her mobile phone or perhaps to check her e-mails. Clive wished that he could become more enthusiastic about the new technology. The previous week he had posted a card to an old friend, knowing it would take two days to travel fifty miles; at the same time Charlotte had sent a text message to a friend in Dubai and received a reply within two minutes.

Feeling unwanted in this company, he sought sanctuary in his study and distraction with the morning newspaper, which could

241

always be relied upon to find somebody less fortunate than himself. In France a man had driven 500 miles with his dead wife sitting beside him. He said he hadn't noticed as the radio was on loud.

The study door opened and Holly came in.

'I've rung my mother,' she said.

'Oh?'

'We're moving out. I can't live here in this atmosphere.'

It took him a moment to grasp what she was saying. The last thing he expected was that she would go. She had made it very clear yesterday that she wouldn't. His refusal to move out himself after hearing about the Brad episode had obviously changed things, but if she was going to leave he would not have expected her to go to her mother's.

Granny Hucknall was a morose old bat who had lost her husband in a freak accident on a golf course (hearing the shout of 'Fore!' he had wittily shouted 'Five!' before the ball struck him on the temple) and she now clung to the lifebelt of religion with the zeal of an archbishop. Clive, who believed that religion was the root of all evil, couldn't understand why tragedy turned people towards God when he would have expected it to turn them away.

He said to Holly, 'It's your decision, not mine.'

'Well, it wouldn't be yours, would it?' she replied in gelid tones. 'You never make a decision.'

'I used to,' he said, 'but you always overruled me.' The duty he felt to dissuade her from leaving was undermined by the certain knowledge that she didn't actually like him. 'When are you going?'

'Now. In a minute. I've just got to tell Charlotte.'

She left the room without bothering to shut the door, and he got up and shut it himself. The newspaper no longer held his attention. He imagined his wife and daughter arriving at Granny Hucknall's semi-detached in Bath with a Range Rover full of suitcases, and wondered doubtfully whether Holly would find a better atmosphere there. And if she didn't, what would happen then? The money Brad had given them was in a joint account, and he could see most of it vanishing as Holly found that it was necessary to buy a new house.

The door burst open and Charlotte rushed in, tears streaming down her face. She threw her arms round Clive's neck.

'I'm sorry, Daddy. I'm sorry. I don't want to go and live with Granny Hucknall. I want to stay here!'

He hugged her and said nothing. She seemed to have no idea of the damage she had done.

'I love this new house!' she cried. 'I hate Granny Hucknall. She mings.'

Clive continued to hug her. She was shaking with sobs. He could see that to be banged up with a demented old crone who was apt to rhapsodize about 'the risen Christ' every ten minutes was not what she would choose, but it was less harmful company than she would have chosen herself.

'I did warn you, darling,' he said, 'that Mummy would be upset if you told her. Well, now she is.'

'I was ill! I didn't know what I was saying! You were right about drugs!'

The recantation was welcome but too late. He told her sadly, 'There's nothing I can do.'

'Yes, there is! You can persuade Mummy to stay here.'

'And do you think she'll listen? It's too late now. You've done the damage. Your mother is a very determined lady.'

'Well, can't I stay here?'

The idea took Clive by surprise, and flattered him. 'Of course you can. This is your home. But you'll have to get your mother's agreement.'

How unlikely this was became apparent

immediately as Holly reappeared at the door.

'Charlotte, have you finished packing?' she called.

'I'm going to stay here,' she said, wiping her eyes.

'You most definitely aren't,' Holly said, marching in. 'Get upstairs. Pack what you can, and leave what you can't.' She turned to Clive. 'You could help carry cases.'

She took Charlotte's arm, and dragged her sobbing daughter from the room. The concern of less than forty-eight hours ago that she might be dying seemed to have been forgotten. Clive followed them upstairs and collected two hefty suitcases, which he carried down to the hall. Then he went up again and fetched two more. It didn't look as if Holly would be leaving very much.

An hour later, the packing completed, the three of them gathered in the hall. Holly was ice cold, Clive was embarrassed, Charlotte was crying. After the abuse that had been thrown around this house recently, Clive was lost for words.

'Will you be OK?' he tried.

Holly was standing alongside their old longcase clock, a wedding present from her uncle. It seemed an inappropriate backdrop for her departure.

'It will be like shedding a skin,' she replied.

Clive was more concerned about Charlotte. The venom had gone, but whether it was the result of the stay in hospital or this new domestic upheaval he couldn't tell.

'Mummy says I can't take my computer,' she said.

'Mother doesn't hold with computers,' Holly said briskly.

'I'll look after it for you,' Clive promised. He gave her a kiss. 'I'm thrilled that you're feeling better. You had us both worried there.'

'I'm sorry, Dad,' she said. She seemed utterly defeated. Clive consoled himself with the thought that Granny Hucknall was most unlikely to roll her a joint.

He carried the cases out to the Range Rover in an atmosphere of sepulchral gloom, and then stood in the drive watching as Holly drove slowly away. Charlotte, in the front seat beside her, had buried her face in a handkerchief. Perhaps one day, he thought, he would be able to tell her that if she hadn't told the story of Sandra, Holly would not have gone to bed with Brad.

20

Clare stood in the garden holding an artist's pad in one hand and a thick black pencil in the other. A twenty-foot tape measure, neatly rolled, lay at her feet.

'I'm getting nervous about Meadow Way,' she said. 'As far as I can see, you're the only husband who hasn't strayed.' It was two days since Holly had decamped in a haze of vitriol, dragging her weeping daughter with her.

'Too tired,' said Andy. 'The writing takes it out of you.'

It had certainly taken it out of him. He felt exhausted, but the story was coming along well. Luke was now playing in the Premier League, scoring goals with nonchalant effrontery from the halfway line when he could avoid the fearsome lunges of envious opponents who seemed determined to cripple him. Writing it plunged Andy into a wonderful fantasy world: he had always wanted to score goals like this himself.

But he was glad to be hauled from his desk, summoned by his wife into sunshine that made him blink, to hear her plans for the garden while Greg completed a series of circuits on his new bike. A pebble mosaic patio had come with the house, but beyond that there was only half an acre of rough grass that demanded creative attention. It was this challenge that Clare had happily accepted, and after her triumph with the pergola Andy was happy to leave her to it. He had thought they might have to hire a company of landscapers, but when he looked at her pad he could see that this would not be necessary.

Halfway up on the left she had a small swimming pool (with blue ceramic tiles, underlined), and at the top an octagonal cedar summerhouse, with tiled floor, seats and cushions. Here, surrounded by flowers and foliage, she planned to read novels or watch Greg swim in the pool. Aromatic herbs, including rosemary, would fill the air with a wonderful smell. She said that she could do without the ornaments — the sculpted cat or the garden gnome — but fancied a hot tub in the vicinity of the pool. Banks of her beloved hydrangeas would provide some privacy on one side, and a screen of bamboo canes would serve the same purpose on the other. Nearer the house, not far from the patio, Andy saw on her drawing a brick-built barbecue.

'It's wonderful,' he said.

'The garden's west-facing, so we're going

to be sunny for most of the day,' she told him. She kicked the rough grass. 'We'll dig this stuff up and lay a proper lawn.'

'Who will?' asked Andy.

'People you're going to hire.'

Greg, tired of his circuits, pulled up alongside them. 'They said on the radio that migrating birds are going to return to Britain earlier this year because of the mild weather,' he said. 'How did they hear about it?'

'The little bastard's got us again,' said Andy. 'Where does he get these questions from? Hey, Greg. If one synchronized swimmer drowns, do the rest have to?'

Greg's expression suggested that if this was the best his father could do he was a serious disappointment. Instead, he asked, 'When are we going to have neighbours?'

'Quite soon, I think,' Andy told him. The previous day he had spied from a window as a family was shown round number 4. He was sorry to see that it was an elderly man with a grey-haired wife and a son in his twenties — a playmate for Greg was what he had hoped for — but probably you had to he getting on a bit to be able to afford these houses.

The only neighbour he had left appeared at that moment in the next garden, head down, hands plunged deep in his pockets, as he shuffled along the unkempt grass in a slow, thoughtful walk.

'Invite him to dinner,' Clare suggested. 'The poor sod can't cook, apparently.'

Clive reached the end of the garden and turned before he noticed them.

'What are you doing?' Andy asked.

'Getting some air.' His face was pale and tired, and the smile of greeting which the situation seemed to call for didn't arrive.

'My wife wonders whether you'd care to dine with us?'

The faintest smile now appeared. 'That would be terrific.'

Half an hour later, washed, changed and refreshed, he turned up at the front door and they took him in and deposited him in an armchair.

'I had a hell of a phone call from Charlotte,' he said miserably. 'The poor girl was practically in hysterics.'

'What's the matter with her?' Clare asked.

'Oh I don't know. Granny Hucknall won't let her play her music. And then there's grace before every meal.'

Clive was clearly upset, but it was not a feeling that Clare shared. Her disapproval of Charlotte had grown with each new item of news she had heard. The Ecstasy and the cannabis in the bedroom horrified her, and she blamed the girl, with her wilful story-telling, for Holly's behaviour with Brad and the destruction of the marriage.

'That's not too big an ordeal, is it?' she said. 'Grace before meals?'

'It appears to put a damper on things.'

'You seem to have forgiven her, Clive?'

'Of course I've forgiven her. She's my daughter. She's only a girl. I'm bloody sorry for her, as a matter of fact. She's missing all her friends.'

'The friends she had, it's a good miss,' said Clare. 'What's going to happen about her exams?'

'Bath's got schools. Holly's got to find one.'

'Well, there you are then,' said Andy in a forlorn attempt to cheer up his disconsolate visitor. 'She'll make new friends and be OK.'

'She won't be OK,' said Clive adamantly. 'She hasn't got her computer, so she can't e-mail anybody, and the money's run out on her mobile phone. Holly can't renew it because her mother doesn't like mobile phones.'

'They won't be staying with your mother-in-law for ever, will they? Holly, presumably, will buy a house.'

'And then I'll be broke,' said Clive.

Clare stood up. 'I've got to get dinner. Why

don't you take our glum guest out for a drink?'

★ ★ ★

Outside, Clive confessed that to ease his distress he had taken a couple of whiskies so it was decided that Andy should drive. In the pub, his distress not entirely alleviated, Clive had another.

'Make it a large one,' he told Eddie, 'and have one yourself.' He sat on his stool, which never seemed the right pew for his long limbs. There wasn't an ounce of fat on him, and his eyes were slightly red, but whether from tiredness or tears Andy couldn't guess.

What he regarded as the inflexible law of pubs, that the least interesting person will talk the most and the most interesting person will talk the least, was in force: a man nearby was describing how you took the gearbox out of a Cortina.

Andy drank lager, and wondered what he could do to prevent this little pub visit from turning into a wake. Of course Brad should be here too. He had bought the houses to bring them back together, and now they were drinking without him.

'There is one consolation,' said Clive when he had finished half of his large whisky. 'I shall be able to vote in a general election without knowing that my vote is being cancelled out by my wife.'

'That's right. Look on the bright side,' said Andy. 'No more midnight dashes to hospital to see your drugged daughter.' But Clive looked so upset by this remark that he realized he had said the wrong thing.

'I'm worried about that girl,' he said. His hands, briefly released from drink-holding duties, were folded submissively in his lap. 'I've let her down.'

'How have you let her down?' Andy asked, anxious to dispel this fresh eruption of guilt. 'What more could you have done?'

'I could have made her a better person with more diligent guidance,' Clive pronounced solemnly.

'Bollocks,' Andy replied. 'By the time she was thirteen all the influences were coming from elsewhere.'

'She could have dealt with those if I'd done my job properly,' said Clive, and then suddenly lost interest in what he was saying. His face was fixed on the door of the bar, and the sadness which had taken up residence in his pale face dropped away.

'It's Sandra!' he said.

Andy was surprised that this arrival caused so much pleasure. The last time Sandra appeared, Clive was practically hiding under his stool.

'Is that good?' he asked.

'It's very good,' said Clive firmly. Sandra spotted them immediately and came over. She was wearing a smart peach shirt with many undone buttons at the top, and a tight black skirt that just reached her knees now but wouldn't if she sat down.

'Hi, Clive,' she said.

Clive smiled happily at the greeting. Their relationship, which had begun with intimacy and then swung to formality, was now swinging back again.

'Miss Deacon, it's a pleasure to feast my eyes on your svelte figure,' he said, and kissed her hand. Looking at her receptive smile, Andy decided that this chivalrous gesture was as superfluous as foreplay to a duck.

'He's pissed,' he told her. 'He's two diamonds short of a tiara at the moment.'

'Poor Clive,' said Sandra. 'What's eating you?'

'There's been some downsizing in the domestic infrastructure,' Clive said.

'He means his wife's buggered off,' Andy explained.

'Oh, how awful!' exclaimed Sandra rapturously. 'Do you think she'll come back?'

'I doubt it,' said Clive. 'Somebody told her

about our amatory experience on the office furniture.'

'He means the bonk on the desk,' said Andy.

'Sandra doesn't need subtitles, Andy,' said Clive irritably. 'She's a woman of intelligence and sophistication. She's a lap dancer.' He picked up his whisky and looked into her eyes. He thought that after the cautious and respectable life he had led, this down-to-earth bundle was just what he needed.

'A lap dancer?' said Andy. 'Let me buy you a drink. I've never met one before.'

'A fruit juice,' said Sandra. 'I'm driving.'

'I thought you were a cleaner?'

'Sandra is just like you,' said Clive. 'She never stops working. The only difference is she gets paid for it.'

She was looking at Clive as if he embodied all those attributes and qualities that made certain film stars irresistible to thousands of women. Failing to spot these characteristics himself, Andy wondered about the magical powers of Viagra.

'What are you going to do?' Sandra asked.

'I shall pick myself up from this reverse and start a new life,' Clive declared.

'That's the way! When my husband left me I threw a party.'

'You were married?' asked Clive.

255

'That's how I come to have a daughter of fifteen. Her father was a very talented rock musician.'

'What happened to him?'

'He had a weakness for groupies, and one of them took him away. He's in America now, according to cards he sends Rebecca.'

'Would I have heard of him?'

'Probably, but I can't bring myself to pronounce his name.'

'I can't even remember my wife's name. Molly? Polly? Dolly?'

'Holly,' said Andy.

'That's it. Prickly stuff, holly.'

The atmosphere between them was becoming so cosy that Andy was beginning to feel like an intruder. He was keen to learn about the mechanics of lap dancing, but contributions to the conversation from him were not wanted.

After a while he looked at his watch.

'I don't want to rain on the parade,' he said, 'but we ought to be getting back. Dinner will be ready.'

'Include me out,' said Clive.

'What?'

'I shall have to forgo your generous offer. My apologies to Clare.'

'She won't be very pleased,' Andy warned him.

'You know what they say. Enjoy yourself; it's later than you think.'

'Good night, Andy,' said Sandra.

★ ★ ★

'What do you mean, Clive's not coming?' asked Clare. 'I've cooked him a beautiful Dover sole.'

'We met Sandra in the pub.'

'Sandra, the amenable cleaning lady?'

'That's her. You know what he said at his birthday party. Life is short and you might as well concentrate on enjoying yourself because nobody is going to admire you for your sacrifices and self-restraint. It looks as if he meant it.'

'What a family,' said Clare angrily as she handed them the fish she had carefully prepared. 'The dad's off with the cleaner, the mum's in bed with the neighbour, and the daughter's in hospital drugged up to the eyeballs.'

'Can I have his Dover sole?' Greg asked.

'I'll share it with you,' Andy said, pouring wine.

'I shan't invite him to dinner again,' said Clare, and Andy could see that she was quietly furious at Clive's non-appearance.

'Don't get cross, Mummy,' said Greg. 'He's a sad case.'

'A sad case?' asked Andy, interested in this display of sympathy.

'Well, he's lost his job and his wife and his daughter. How sad is that?'

'You're a kind boy, Greg,' said Clare, calming down. 'But you've never cooked a Dover sole.'

'It's all right for you two,' Greg explained patiently. 'You're in love.'

'You know a lot,' Andy said. 'Let me tell you something you don't know. When I got engaged to your mother, I'd never spoken to her.'

Greg paused at this, examining the puzzle. 'Oh God — you didn't meet on the internet, did you?'

'I don't think there was an internet then,' Clare told him. 'It was much more romantic than that.'

Greg's curiosity increased. 'How can it have been romantic if he didn't speak to you?'

Clare gave Andy a smile, and it took him right back to the day they had met in a bookshop where he was signing paperback copies of *Raging Hormones*. He found these excursions to the front deeply embarrassing, but was encouraged by his publisher to come out of hiding and help the sales graph. The queue didn't exactly go out into the street, but there were always enough buyers around to keep him reasonably busy. Several were anxious to let him know that they weren't buying the book for themselves, and asked him to sign the copy they had bought for somebody else. He always signed 'best wishes' followed by whatever name he was told, but that day a vision appeared before him with a flower in her black hair, a white dress, and eyes that hypnotized him. He stared at her and forgot to ask her name, but she had seen the way it worked with the previous customer and so she said 'Clare' and pointed at the book. Andy came out of his daze and wrote in his best writing: *Marry me, Clare. Andy Devlin.* He shut the book and handed it to her, but she left the shop without reading it as other customers moved towards him clutching his precious paperback. When the stint had finished, he rushed into the street, hoping to catch a glimpse of her, but she was nowhere to be seen. And then, as he walked with a terrible feeling of emptiness back to the little Peugeot that had been provided by his book money, she jumped out of a car parked not far away and walked towards him with a lovely smile. 'I've just read your message,' she said. 'The answer's yes.' He was engaged to a girl he had never spoken to! He had never heard of anything so romantic. It was mid-afternoon, so he took her to an expensive, old-fashioned restaurant for tea and fancy cakes. While elderly waitresses in starched white pinafores lingered respectfully around them, Andy was confirmed in his suspicion that he had found somebody special, and an hour later, to show he meant what he said, they were in a jeweller's shop looking at engagement rings. He was in a hurry now (she might lose her nerve) and he believed in the old saying about too long a courtship spoiling the marriage. The wedding took place four months later. It was 1990. He didn't mind that marriage was out that year. So was everything else. Mandela was let out, Thatcher was kicked out, and England were knocked out — of the World Cup. But for Andy 1990 was a year to remember for a quite different reason.

Greg, who had arrived two years later, listened to this story with undisguised pleasure.

'I bet he put an 'i' in Clare,' he said.

'As a matter of fact he didn't,' Clare told him. 'I was very impressed.'

'It was a fifty-fifty chance, but it was my lucky day,' Andy explained.

'And then you had me,' Greg announced with a broad smile.

'Well, no run of luck lasts for ever,' replied Andy, and Greg's serviette came flying across the table and landed on his head.

'You look like Yasser Arafat,' Greg decided.

★ ★ ★

When Clive woke up the following morning he found himself staring at pink and grey striped wallpaper he had never seen before. I've been kidnapped, he thought. There was a hand in his groin which he was fairly certain wasn't his, and he wasn't wearing his pyjamas. A faint throbbing at the front of his head impeded the immediate task of unravelling these mysteries, but he closed his eyes again and tried to remember what had happened.

'I've got to go to work,' said Sandra's voice beside him, and it began to come back.

'This may sound a silly question,' he said, 'but where are we?'

'A place called London,' Sandra said. She swung her legs out of the bed, but then sat there as if a small rest would be needed before any further progress could be made.

Clive studied her naked back. It was slim and smooth and he reached out to touch it. 'Anywhere in particular?' he asked.

'Southampton Row. Very central.'

'And do I gather that this is your flat?'

'I own it, thanks to the royalties from some

old hit record. Look, what are you going to do? I've got to go to that office you used to work in.'

He looked up at the surprisingly high ceiling. His body wanted to get up, but his brain preferred the warm comfort of his pillow. 'I think I'll stay here,' he said. 'What happened last night?'

'Well, when we went to leave the Hen and Chicken you remembered that you didn't have any transport, so I gave you a lift. I had to get back to London for work this morning and you decided to come with me. You kept saying that there was nobody at home and you'd be lonely.'

'God, I'd forgotten. My family left me.'

'Apparently,' said Sandra. 'I'll make you a cup of tea.' She put on a pink shortie housecoat and left him in bed. His thoughts flew to Bath as he tried to imagine Granny Hucknall, Holly and a surly Charlotte trying to enjoy breakfast together. But when he looked at his watch he saw that it was only half past six. Sandra's job had an early start.

She returned with a cup of tea for him and sat on the bed. 'Stay here today,' she said. 'Please. I'll be home by four and we can go out for a meal. It's a non-dancing day. If you want to go out I'll leave keys on the kitchen table, and you'll find food in the fridge.'

Clive lay on his back thinking of the everyday items that were no longer within his reach — clean shirts, socks, his razor and toothbrush, his car. But then he thought: I'm forty, and I decided to enjoy my life. The job had gone, so there was no work to do. The family had gone, so they obviously didn't require his care and attention. Sacrifice and self-restraint were yesterday's idea. Here was a new chance, perhaps a new life, no matter how strange it seemed at the moment.

'I'll be here when you get back,' he promised.

21

The polished white saloon car that pulled smoothly into her drive would have been regarded by Olivia as an elegant addition to the scenery but for one disquieting feature — the one-word notice, POLICE, that squatted transversely across the roof. She looked from an upstairs window at the two uniformed occupants who were conferring over a sheet of paper and seemed in no hurry to get out.

Instinctively she looked for Brad. He wasn't easy to find as he had fallen asleep on the sofa and sunk below her field of vision from the door. An open newspaper lay across his chest. Olivia had never approved of sleeping during the day.

'Wake up,' she said.

Brad stirred. 'I wasn't asleep. I was studying the inside of my eyelids.'

'And that made you snore, did it?'

'My biorhythms collapse after lunch and I need a snooze.' He sat up, aware of disapproval.

'You've got visitors,' Olivia told him. 'Two of them.'

Brad got reluctantly to his feet, and saw the police car through the window.

'Police? What do they want? You paid the TV licence, didn't you?'

The two policemen had now climbed out of the car and were making their way towards the front door. Brad went to open it.

'Bradley Rowe?' asked one of them. He was wearing a cap and was clearly the senior partner here. The other was a burly police constable. Mind and muscle. 'I wonder if we might come in?'

'Is it necessary?' Brad asked. He was still half asleep, and in no mood to entertain anyone.

'It would be best, sir,' said the officer. 'These things are best discussed inside. We have a warrant here for your arrest.'

Olivia, loitering in the background, pushed herself into view on hearing this. 'A warrant for his arrest? What on earth are you talking about?'

'Some cock-up in Noddy land,' said Brad. 'Yes, you'd better come in.'

He showed the policemen into the sitting room, but nobody sat down.

'What's this all about?' Brad asked. He wanted to clear the matter up and get rid of this couple as soon as possible, but the next remark from the police officer went in like a knife, and told him that the situation would not develop in that direction.

'What this is all about, sir, is a Bentley Turbo RT. Registration number BR40. Acting on information received from a Mr Jeremy Rowe — Rowe? Relative of yours, is he?'

'Cousin.'

'Acting on information received from Mr Rowe, Dorset police dug up a field on a farm and found the car had been buried — the car you claimed to have been stolen.'

'It *was* stolen!' cried Olivia, from whose face all colour had now gone. 'It was stolen from here in the middle of the night!'

'You're saying that some thief stole your car from here and drove it down to Dorset and buried it in your cousin's field?'

'No,' said Brad. 'You're telling us that.'

'We understand that you received a cheque for £30,000 from the insurers?'

'I did.'

'The car was stolen!' shouted Olivia. She still didn't understand what was happening. 'No wonder all the car thieves get away with it. You don't even recognize a theft when it's under your nose.'

'The courts will decide that, madam,' said the police officer politely. 'That's what they're for.' He was a tall, good-looking man with intelligent eyes that had the faintly world-weary look which told you he had been listening to lies for years. He turned to Brad. 'If you've nothing else to say, sir, I think we might as well get on with it.'

Brad stood in the middle of the room in a state of shock wondering what exactly he could say. He was aware now that any remark could subsequently be shown to hold a significance he hadn't intended, and that in his situation silence was usually the best strategy.

'I want to see my solicitor,' he said.

'All in good time, sir,' said the officer. 'But first I am arresting you on the charge of defrauding the Westhay Insurance Company of £30,000. You don't have to say any-thing — '

'I've heard that line on television,' said Brad.

'This is disgraceful,' Olivia burst out. 'I'm going to contact my MP.'

'I shouldn't bother, madam,' said the officer helpfully. 'We're arresting him this evening on an indecency charge. Distasteful episode in a public lavatory, apparently.'

An appreciative guffaw at this riposte came from the police constable, but was cut short by a glance from the officer.

'And what about Jeremy?' Brad asked. 'Are

you prosecuting him?'

'No, sir. He's our chief witness.'

'I see.'

Olivia sat down, trying to assimilate the size of the disaster she was watching. An arrested husband would lose her all her friends and destroy her formidable social aspirations. She struggled to convince herself that the matter would be resolved and the nightmare would soon end, and then she heard Brad say something stupid and she knew with a chilling certainty that he was guilty.

'Look, I won the Lottery a few weeks ago,' he said. 'Why don't I write you both a big cheque?'

'You're looking at a four-year sentence, Mr Rowe,' the officer said coldly. 'If you want to double it by trying to bribe a police officer, that's up to you.'

'Anyway,' said the police constable, who evidently had a sense of humour, 'you can't bribe two policemen at the same time. You have to approach them individually.'

'I'll try to remember that,' said Brad.

'Shall we go?' said the officer.

Brad went across to Olivia and gave her a kiss.

'Can I come?' she asked.

'I'm afraid not,' the officer told her. 'Your

husband can get in touch with you later.'

As Olivia collapsed on the sofa in tears, the three men left the room.

★ ★ ★

At that moment Clive was speeding westward on the M4 and trying to weigh in his mind the attractions of the ancient city of Bath against the dismal prospect of meeting the repellent Granny Hucknall. The Georgian terraces, crescents and squares had provided him with a pleasant escape on his infrequent visits to his mother-in-law, when he would leave his wife with her mother and wander off to enjoy the Roman baths, the loveliest street in Europe and the only bridge in England that had shops on it. Bath, named 1,500 years ago by the West Saxons, had become a centre for fashionable society in the eighteenth century. What Granny Hucknall was doing there was beyond his comprehension.

She greeted him with glacial indifference, not even managing to speak. She was wearing a thick black roll-neck sweater and brown corduroy trousers.

'I've come to see Holly,' he said.

She stood in the doorway, blocking any possibility of entrance, and looked him up and down as if his choice of clothing defied belief.

'I don't think she wants to see you, does she?' she said in her reedy voice.

'OK. Charlotte then,' said Clive.

Granny Hucknall was considering how best to resist this request when Charlotte appeared behind her.

'I thought I heard your voice,' she said. 'What are you doing here, Daddy?'

'Hallo, dear,' he said. 'I came to see your mother, but it seems — '

'I'll get her,' said Charlotte, and disappeared down the long narrow hallway which was all you could see from the door. His mother-in-law continued to stare at him, but abandoned the vigil when Holly appeared.

'Well,' she said. It seemed to fall halfway between a question and an expression of surprise.

Clive, pointed at her departing mother. 'How does she reconcile her Christian beliefs with that naked hatred?'

'Don't ask,' said Holly. 'Why are you here?'

'I've come to offer you the house. You can go home.'

'And where will you be?'

'Somewhere else.'

She gave him a long, cool look while she took this in. There was no indication that she was pleased. 'I suppose you were scared that I'd have to buy a house?' she suggested.

'Don't look a gift horse in the mouth, Holly,' he said sadly. There was no placating the Hucknall women.

'I won't,' she said. 'I'll pack my stuff.'

'When will you move?'

'Now.' She turned to Charlotte, who was standing behind her. 'Get packing. We're going home.'

'Yippee,' said Charlotte. Suddenly she was smiling.

Holly turned back to Clive. 'Perhaps you'll help me load the car? You can come in and wait.'

'And chat to your mother? I'd sooner eat crud.'

'I'll get rid of her.'

'Strychnine's good,' said Clive, and was finally admitted to the house. He followed Holly down the hall and into the room at the end, which they called the parlour. There was a stale smell as if the windows were never opened, and the furniture was old and bruised. Holly and Charlotte went upstairs to pack, taking Granny Hucknall with them. Left on his own, Clive looked round at the cheerless living space. On a small wooden table there was a pile of magazines, all with Christian or church in the title. There was a two-bar electric fire, some plastic daffodils, a medicine bottle, a half-eaten bar of chocolate, but no television. On the mantelpiece was a fading photograph of a grim-looking Arthur Hucknall who had fatally opted for the challenge of the golf course as an escape from this sombre Victorian environment. He had always shown a strange sympathy towards Clive, which he only now understood: he knew what Clive was letting himself in for.

After half an hour he stood up, deciding that another look at Bath's architecture would be a better way of using this wasted time, when Holly came in wearing pale blue jeans, a scoop-neck T-shirt, and a new expression of impregnable self-satisfaction.

'Hit the road, Jack,' she said. 'Another week here and I'd have worked out how to garrotte myself with a shoe lace.' This was as cheerful as Clive had seen her for some time, but he found it hard to share the excitement: he had no part in it.

'I'll fetch the cases,' he said.

Charlotte was coming downstairs looking equally buoyant, despite the luggage she was carrying. 'Thanks, Dad,' she said, and gave him a kiss on the cheek.

He went into the bedroom that Holly always used and started to carry suitcases down. There was no sign of his mother-in-law. Perhaps she was praying.

When the Range Rover was loaded he sat in his Rover while Holly and Charlotte went in to say goodbye. Then he followed his wife's car as they headed north in search of the M4. He could only imagine the jubilation in the vehicle in front.

Two hours later they pulled into Meadow Way. Clive had come to help them unload, but there were also one or two of his own possessions that he wanted to collect.

Olivia and Clare were standing on the doorstep next door. Clare smiled and waved at this unexpected return, but Olivia seemed to be crying.

'You're coming back?' Clare called, as Holly got out of the car.

'Some of us are,' said Holly cheerfully. 'What's the matter with Olivia? Is she sorry to see us?'

Clare came over to them. 'Something terrible's happened. Brad's been arrested.'

★   ★   ★

Brad had never liked police stations. He didn't even like uniforms and was suspicious of people who chose to wear one. What sad soul was the camouflage concealing?

273

They ushered him into an office at the back of the station where an officer more senior than those who had called at his house sat in a resplendent uniform at a large modern desk. The implication, that £30,000 insurance frauds were on a more serious level than the vandalism and petty larcenies which occupied inferior station staff, was clear enough. Brad stared balefully at his new exalted inquisitor who he realized was a chief inspector. In this Pirandello-like setting he might have displayed his insouciant side, but he had heard the fearful words 'four years' back at his house, and the seriousness of his situation had now sunk in. Anxious to gabble, he managed to stay mute.

'Mr Rowe, there are various issues we have to resolve,' said the chief inspector, studying a pile of paperwork in front of him. 'This isn't a trivial matter.'

'I want my solicitor here,' Brad said.

The chief inspector pushed a sheet of paper in front of him and handed him a Parker pen. 'Write his name on there.'

The sheet was passed to a constable who had been standing at the side of the room with his hands behind his back. He left the room and returned a few minutes later.

'He'll be here in an hour, sir,' he said.

'An hour?' said the chief inspector. 'Well,

Mr Rowe can't sit here for an hour. Put him in the pen.'

Brad was now provided with the company of two policemen who led him down endless flights of stairs while discussing a football match played the previous evening. They came into a large bare room with a cement floor. At one end were three cells, but to one side there was a cage-like structure with a table and chairs in it. A man sat on one of the chairs with his head on the table, presumably asleep. One of the policemen unlocked the door and motioned to Brad to go in.

'How long is this for?' he asked.

'Not long. You've got to wait somewhere until your brief shows,' the policeman replied.

Brad went in and sat down, hearing for the first time a door being locked behind him. It was not something that he liked, and a real sense of alarm gripped him now. Nobody had ever had power over him like this.

The other man stirred, woken by the noise. It was Jason Marr.

'We can't go on meeting like this,' said Brad.

'Christ!' Jason Marr moaned. 'It's that boring fatty from the wine bar. What they banged you up for?' He was busily arranging his blond ponytail, which was not hanging properly after his sleep on the table. He seemed to be wearing the same yellow T-shirt.

'It's a misunderstanding,' said Brad.

'Oh yeah. I've had lots of those.'

'Why are you here this time?'

'I think the charge is possessing a class-A drug with intent to supply. They caught me with a tin of thirty-six Ecstasy tablets. I'm looking at four months.'

A few weeks ago Brad would have regarded Marr as a villain. Now Marr was 'looking at' four months, when he was 'looking at' four years. Nothing brought the depth of his fall home to him more graphically.

He asked, 'You've been to prison before?'

'Once or twice.'

'What's the worst part?'

Marr had no doubt. 'Violent prisoners.'

Until the last hour Brad had never given prison much thought, but it was looming large in his imagination now and he didn't like what Jason Marr had told him. He went back in his mind to the circumstances that had brought him here, and realized that a million to Jeremy would have avoided it all. If Olivia hadn't just asked for a million for her miserable family, he would probably have lent it to him.

'Were you a one-man operation?' he asked Marr. Their situation demanded a conversation of some sort.

276

'I am now. My partner scarpered with the dosh. What was your game? Smuggling?'

'Public relations.'

'Oh yeah? What did you publicly relate?'

'Good news.'

'Overpaid ventriloquist,' said Marr contemptuously.

'Thanks,' said Brad, looking at his watch. 'Tell me about that parrot again. I could do with a laugh.'

The two policemen appeared an hour later. One of them unlocked the door. 'Your lawyer's here,' he said, beckoning to Brad.

'What about me?' asked Jason Marr.

'Your moment will come, sunshine,' said the policeman, locking the door on him.

Marcus was waiting upstairs with a large smile and a shiny black briefcase. He was a short, bright man of about thirty, with greased black hair. He had successfully represented Brad's firm in several legal squabbles, but had not been called on before to act for him in a personal case.

'What have you been up to, Brad?' he asked.

'Nothing.'

'And they locked you up for it? That's disgraceful!' He gave Brad a wink. 'Let's go and see the chief and see how the land lies.'

'Your wife rang,' the chief inspector said

when they went into his office. 'Noisy lady, isn't she?'

Brad didn't answer. He was looking at the desk between them, on which lay several photographs of his car being lifted by crane from the tomb that Jeremy had created for it.

'Your client has been charged with defrauding the Westhay Insurance Company of £30,000,' the chief inspector told Marcus. 'The car he reported stolen has been found, as you can see from these photographs, buried on his cousin's farm in Dorset.'

Marcus picked up the photographs and studied them. 'My client doesn't wish to say anything at the moment,' he said. 'The only subject we want to raise is bail.'

'He won't get it today,' said the chief inspector. 'But we'll have him in court tomorrow for a remand hearing, and you can see what the magistrates say.'

'You mean I'm going to spend a night in the cells?' Brad asked.

'I'm afraid so,' said the chief inspector. 'They're very comfortable, I'm told.'

Brad could see a headline before his eyes as clearly as if the newspaper had already been printed: PR BOSS JAILED FOR FRAUD.

'My client needs to talk to his wife,' Marcus announced now. 'I'd be much obliged if you'd arrange a phone call.'

He was left alone with a phone in a small office next door. He had no doubt that his call would be recorded. In fact, when he got home — if he ever got home — the phone there would probably be bugged as well.

Olivia was frantic. 'What's going on, Brad?' she sobbed. 'I really can't take much more!' As these were only the opening hours in what was obviously going to be an ongoing nightmare, Brad felt that his wife had reached exhaustion point rather early.

'They're going to keep me in tonight. There'll be a court hearing in the morning when I should get bail,' he told her.

'Are they going to put you in a cell?'

'Well, I don't think they're going to offer the Waldorf bloody Astoria.'

'Oh, Brad! What can we do?'

'What you can do is get round here with my razor et cetera. Anything you think I'll need. I don't want to show up in court tomorrow looking like a tramp.'

After he had ended the call, he phoned Andy.

'Have you ever stood bail for anyone?' he asked.

* * *

When Andy got back from his phone call he found Holly, wearing an expensive leather and gilt belt, having a cup of tea with Clare in the kitchen.

'We were just saying,' said Holly, 'this three-boys-together project of Brad's isn't panning out too well, is it? One's done a bunk, and another's locked up!'

Andy felt that Holly was deriving some pleasure from this turn of events. It was three-girls-together now.

'That was Brad on the phone,' he said. 'He wants me to go bail for him.'

'How much will it be?' Clare asked.

'His solicitor thinks it could be as high as a hundred thousand.'

'Do you think it's wise?'

'How can I say no? He gave me the money in the first place. Anyway, I won't lose it unless he disappears.'

'Can't he provide his own bail?'

'It's not allowed apparently.'

'Poor Brad,' said Holly. 'Still, he was never hindered by abstract concepts like honesty.'

'Nothing like putting the boot in when a man's down,' said Andy. 'Where's Clive? Vamoosed with a lap dancer, I hear.'

'A lap dancer? Is she really? That will test his resources, such as they are.'

'What about Charlotte?' Clare asked.

'She's thrilled to be back. She's announcing her return to the world with a volley of e-mails.'

'It's Olivia I'm sorry for now,' Clare said.
'I think she's seeing a man.'

'What — all of him?' Andy asked.

'A chap called Mike Flower. Do you know him?'

'I knew a chap at school with that name. He used to masturbate so much he was known as Self-Raising Flower.'

'That must be a different man,' said Holly disdainfully. 'This one's a psychiatrist.'

'What's happening there then?' Clare asked.

'It's her latest fad, but she really needs it. She was talking to him on the phone this afternoon when I went round to sympathize about Brad. I got the impression that it's more than therapy that occurs on the couch.'

'Does she really need therapy?' Clare asked.

'She's wrecked. She's lost all her brownie points with the beau monde.'

'She's also going to lose the company of her husband, but I suppose that isn't so important?' Andy said.

'Women have survived worse,' Holly told him with a smile. Being restored to her lovely home had given her an aggressive edge that he hadn't noticed before. He decided to quit this company and find solace with a book in his study.

Greg was in there, reading. 'Why do people lose their accents when they sing?' he asked.

22

One morning in the supermarket, while Clare was examining vegetables for signs of age and Greg was scanning the shelves for his favourite crisps, Andy, a devotee of the printed word, pulled up alongside the newspapers and magazines that were accorded a privileged position at the front of the store. Old habits died hard: the news could be absorbed here without spending a penny.

Among the periodicals that offered cottages and cruises and cancer cures, he spotted the magazine that had sent the lovely Gaby rushing to Meadow Way with her tiny recording machine and professional curiosity. He picked it up to see what sort of stuff it published. The cover wasn't encouraging. Can a course of jabs hold back the years? Could your destiny lie in your thumbprint? Should my child have bags under his eyes? He opened it and was surprised to find Gaby's article. His photograph reminded him of a rabbit caught in a car's headlights.

His eyes shifted reluctantly to the story she had written. He hated reading about himself, but he forced himself to try a fragment. Gaby liked long sentences.

> His novel of teenage angst and vanishing virginities appeared to grateful applause in the far-off days of 1987 when Britain was still busily re-electing Mrs Thatcher, but despite a monk-like silence on the literary front since then, Devlin, an engagingly modest man, still manages to live in some luxury with a super-dooper six-bedroom house and a Lotus Esprit among other cars in the triple garage. By way of explanation, he cites the legacies of Orwell and Scott Fitzgerald . . .

Too embarrassed to read on, he shut the magazine and returned it to the shelf. His consolation, as usual, was that nobody he knew would see it.

But as he drove home from the supermarket in Clare's new Golf which was better equipped than the now-famous Lotus to carry three people and half a dozen bags of groceries, he felt strangely depressed. Gaby's article had slammed a door on him, placing him firmly in the past. He was a has-been, a forgotten man, scrapheap material at thirty-nine. By the time they reached home with their hoard of food, he had decided that he was metaphorically dead, and his optimistic efforts to create the magical world of Luke and his knee were no more than the posthumous posturings of a literary ghost. He carried the bags inside as the phone started to ring, and he went into his study to take the call.

'Yep?' he said, a subdued greeting from beyond the grave.

'Andy? That you?'

He recognized the throaty voice of Warren Goldberg, and tried to concentrate.

'Hi, Warren. Yes, it's me.'

'Look, Andy. You'd better sit down. It's good news day.'

Andy sat down at his desk. 'Are you sure you've got the right man? I don't get good news.'

'Well, you've got it now, kid. They've gone bananas over your Raleigh script.'

Greg wandered into the room with an atlas. He was studying the book, and didn't notice that his father was on the phone.

'Dad, why do they call it the Middle East? What's it east of? If you're in India, it's in the west. Look at my atlas — '

'Shut up, Greg!' Andy shouted with a frustration he had never shown towards his son before. 'Sorry, Warren. A little interruption from my son here. You were saying?

Something about bananas?'

'You remember that I sent your script to two film companies? Well, they both want it. The first one offered a million dollars, but the second one . . . are you ready for this?'

'Try me.'

'The second offered five million! On your behalf, I accepted immediately.'

Andy, dazed, said, 'That's amazing!'

'Not really. It's all there, you see. The big parts, romance, drama, history. They'll get their writers working on it, call it *Raleigh*, and you'll have an Oscar-winning epic.'

'Good God!' said Andy. 'That's wonderful!' He covered the phone and shouted, 'Clare!'

She came into the room very quickly, and he scribbled on a piece of paper, 'RALEIGH — $5 MILLION!!!!', and handed it to her. She stared at it with eyes that grew ever wider, and then bent to kiss him on the cheek before dancing from the room. He could guess where she was going — in search of champagne.

'You left a bit out, apparently,' Warren was saying. 'Don't worry, they're going to put it in themselves. I've been talking to the director and he's full of ideas. They're going to shoot some of it in South America — '

'What do you mean, left a bit out?'

'They say Raleigh laid his cloak over a

puddle to save the queen from getting her feet wet.'

'I know that, Warren. I just couldn't see a real puddle on a West End stage, and a mock one would have been ridiculous.'

'Don't worry. Hollywood do puddles big time.'

'Oh good.' He could see already that his work would be taken from him, rewritten, expanded, transformed and returned to him as something he barely recognized. And all he would have to comfort himself would be five million dollars! 'You've achieved another miracle, Warren. I can hardly tell you how grateful I am.'

'You did all the work, kid. By the way, the director said if you want to go over with your wife to see some filming it's all expenses paid and you'll be treated like royalty.'

'Clare would love that.'

'The contract is on the way. All you have to do is sign it, and you'll be rich. I'll be in touch soon. I think this calls for another lunch.'

When he had put the phone down, Andy sat at his desk for a few moments and thought about what he had been told. There were, he realized, tears in his eyes. From the kitchen there came the sound of a champagne cork popping, and he stood up and hurried in its direction.

'Isn't that marvellous news?' Clare said. 'Congratulations, darling. I always knew you would do it.'

'I wish I'd known,' said Andy, hugging her. 'It would have made life a lot easier.'

'What happens now?'

'A contract arrives, closely followed by a cheque.'

'For five million dollars!'

'Well, it won't be that much,' Andy had to tell her. 'Warren will take fifteen per cent. It still leaves four and a quarter million. And another thing. We're going to Hollywood to watch some of the filming.'

'I've *always* wanted to go to Hollywood,' Clare said. Her excitement now was so great that she was spilling the champagne as she poured it.

Greg came in. 'Who's going to Hollywood?' he asked.

'You are,' said Andy. 'Sorry I shouted at you, Greg. You were interrupting a man who was telling me that I'd made five million dollars.'

'Wowie! Can I have some roller blades?'

'I think we could manage that, darling,' said Clare.

When the champagne had gone and they were all trying to calm down from the shock, Andy returned to his study and struggled to take in the sensational leap that his life had just made. It was impossible to concentrate on the story of Luke. Instead he pulled out the script that had produced this miraculous amount of money, and read it through. His last line was Raleigh's brave last line.

RALEIGH
I have a long journey to take, and must bid the company farewell.

Since finishing the play Andy had found that many other 'last words' were attributed to Walter Raleigh. Just before he was beheaded, he said of the executioner's axe: ' 'Tis a sharp remedy, but a sure cure for all ills.' And then moments later, as he laid his head on the executioner's block, he said: 'So the heart be right, it is no matter which way the head lies.' Perhaps the hungry scriptwriters in Los Angeles would dig up these valedictory gems. He suspected that they would show the execution in gory detail.

His telephone, that bringer of glad tidings, rang again, but this time it was Clive, feeling lonely in his London flat and seeking distant reassurance that he still belonged to the human race.

'As I've got nothing to do and I don't

suppose you have, I thought I'd give you a bell. How are you?'

Andy always resented the assumption of other people that because he was at home he was doing nothing — when the truth was that he rarely left his desk.

'I'm pretty good today,' he said. 'What about you?'

'I'm sitting in this funny little flat with some very old furniture and some strange brown paintings on the wall that seem to be mostly mountains in Nepal or Tibet. From my window I can see the Post Office tower. Later today I shall stroll down to Leicester Square and take in a movie. It's all go!'

Andy pictured this lonely scene and found it depressing. He said, 'Can I ask you a personal question? It's something I'm very curious about.'

'Fire away.'

'How's the romance going in the absence of Viagra?'

'Blimey, I don't need Viagra. Once I've seen Sandy dancing at the club I'm ready for anything.'

'So that's the way it goes.'

Clive shifted gear. 'Listen, have you seen Holly or Charlotte?'

'Clare sees Holly,' Andy told him. 'Apparently Charlotte's acting ambitions are back on course, and the house is drugs-free. I gather your departure shook Charlotte up a bit, or her responsibility for it, and she's starting to concentrate on the things that matter. I don't know much about Holly, but I know she's very relieved to be back in the house.'

'She never liked me, you know,' said Clive. 'She thought I'd provide security and respectability, but she never really fancied me. What about you? What are you up to?'

'As a matter of fact I've just had some amazing news. The Devlin family have been celebrating with champagne.' He told Clive about Warren Goldberg's success with the Raleigh script. 'The first thing I'm going to do when the money arrives is pay back Brad.'

'That's wonderful news, Andy. Congratulations. I shan't be paying Brad back myself, even if I could. I don't feel I owe him much after his little romp with my wife. What's happening to him?'

'He's on bail, but he's heading for prison. Four years seems to be the term he's expecting, which is pretty grim. I can't understand why he did it.'

'Money?' said Clive. 'If only he'd known that a Lottery win was just round the corner. Do you see him much?'

'Not a lot. There was some publicity when

he was remanded and he doesn't like going out. I'm dropping in this afternoon to cheer him up with a game of snooker.'

★ ★ ★

Brad prowled round the snooker table squinting at the balls, hoping to find an alignment that might yield a pot.

'Olivia's having an affair.' he said. 'Preparing herself for my absence, no doubt.'

'Are you sure?' Andy asked. 'She doesn't seem the type.'

'In what way doesn't she seem the type?'

Brad spoke without taking his eyes off the balls. The snooker table was the centre of his life now, and when Andy had gone he would return to it and play on his own.

'Ultra respectable. A great observer of the social conventions.' Andy wanted to imply that Olivia was too snobbish to get laid by anything less than a duke.

'You're half right,' Brad conceded. 'But the daft mare would do it standing up in a canoe with a chap who had the right social background.'

He spotted a red he was happy with and bent over the table. He was wearing what he called his snooker gear — a red sweatshirt with HARVARD on the front, green jeans

291

and Velcro-fastened suede shoes. The ball rolled into a corner pocket with perceptible reluctance, but Brad strolled happily round the table in search of his next shot.

'Who's the man?' Andy asked.

'Her new shrink. Chap called Mike Flower.'

'Upper class, is he?'

'God knows. He's got one of those suntans that looks bloody silly in January. Christmas in the Caribbean, I suppose.'

He hit the cue ball towards the yellow but the white ball went in and the yellow ball stayed out. He retreated from the table, shaking his head in self-reproach, and Andy came up to have a look at the balls.

'You don't seem unduly worried about Mike Flower,' he suggested.

Brad shrugged and sighed. 'What can I do? I'm not going to be here for a long time. I'm sorry for her. She's watching everything disintegrate around her, including me.'

Andy saw a plant and used the spider to pot a red. He found snooker a difficult game. The gulf between a professional player and somebody like him was far bigger than the comparable gulf in any other sport. A footballer could play with a footballer or a cricketer with a cricketer and at least there would be a game, even if you noticed who was inferior, but professional snooker players came from another planet. They made breaks of 100 all the time. Here the score was 12-8 to Brad without a colour being potted. He sought to remedy this and with tremendous concentration potted a brown.

'Are you resigned to four years?' he asked.

'That's what Marcus tells me.'

'If I hadn't stood bail for you, I'd almost suggest you did a bunk.'

Brad sat down as Andy's break was not yet over. 'I've thought about it, to be honest, but I'd spend the rest of my life on the run. And Marcus thinks that four years could be nearer two and a half with remission. The prisons are so full, they're anxious to get rid of you.'

'And then they've got your passport.'

'That doesn't matter. I know a great place in the Isle of Skye.'

'I think you might stand out in the Isle of Skye, particularly as your picture would be in all the papers.'

He potted a red and then a blue, giving him a break of eleven. It was nearly his record. But when he tried to improve on it the red rattled in a corner pocket and wouldn't go in. Brad came to the table and stared at the balls as if he had never seen such an unfortunate arrangement on the green baize before.

Andy stood and watched him. He wanted to tell him about his good fortune with the Raleigh project, but was unsure how to approach it. Somebody else's good news was difficult to listen to, let alone celebrate, when you were mired in the misery that enveloped Brad.

'I'm going to pay you back,' he tried. 'The cost of the house and the half million you gave me. It's all coming back to your bank account.'

The news was sufficient to halt Brad in his questing orbit of the balls.

'Oh?' he said. 'How are you going to do that?'

'I had some good news today, Brad. My play about Raleigh has been bought in Hollywood. They're going to make a movie of it.'

'That's bloody wonderful, Andy,' said Brad, genuinely impressed. 'Congratulations!' He insisted on shaking hands, and then asked, 'How much?'

'It starts off as five million dollars, but after my agent has taken his share, and the taxman has taken his share, and the bank have taken their share for converting dollars into sterling, who knows? What's five million dollars in our money, anyway?'

'About three and a half million quid. You've

got a very casual attitude to this new-found wealth, haven't you?'

'It isn't real yet,' Andy admitted. 'But directly it arrives I'll be giving you the cheque.'

'I never intended you to return the money, you know.'

'I know. But now I can, I want to.'

Brad turned back to the table. 'All that scribbling pays off at last! I always suspected it might. The question is, will I be out in time for the premiere?'

'The time they take to make a film, I think you'll be there.'

'I ought to open champagne.'

'We've had champagne,' said Andy, 'but I wouldn't mind a beer.'

Brad disappeared and returned with some bottles of Löwenbräu.

'Heard anything of Clive?' he asked.

Andy was surprised that Brad raised the subject. After his frolic with Holly he thought that Clive might be a subject he would prefer to avoid. 'He phoned this morning, as a matter of fact. I think he's bored. Still, he's got his new girlfriend to keep him young.'

'What did he say?'

'He asked about Holly and Charlotte. And you.'

Brad walked round the table, finding a red

he thought he could pot. 'What did he say about me?'

'I told him I was going to pay you back, and he said he wouldn't be doing the same even if he could. He said that he didn't feel he owed you much after what he called your little romp with his wife.'

'There's an old saying,' said Brad. 'No good deed goes unpunished.'

★ ★ ★

The riverside restaurant they had always wanted to visit but could never afford was twenty miles away. Andy hired a taxi. He had his eye on a bottle or two of Barolo, his favourite Italian wine, and didn't want to leave half a bottle behind just because his Lotus was in the car park waiting to be driven home.

He had reserved a table that overlooked the river in the hope that the boats would distract Greg, who was not old enough to understand that eating out was an extravagant pleasure. They were shown to their coveted corner by a good-looking, young French waiter who flirtatiously paid tribute to Clare's new suit. It was an unusually expensive purchase by her, a consequence of the film deal, and came from one of the world's leading designers whose logo brazenly adorned the jacket.

'I don't want you to look sad tonight,' she said as she opened the ten-page menu. 'We're celebrating.'

'Why should I look sad?'

'Thanks to our debauched neighbours, the three friends together will soon be one.'

'But I got you, babe, as Sonny Bono used to sing.'

'And me,' said Greg. In this ornate Michelin-starred setting he seemed uncommonly shy.

Andy ordered wild duck with a fruity sauce, and warned the waiter that they would be wanting Grand Marnier soufflés later.

'It's very expensive,' said Clare, unused to the prices.

'Well, I haven't come here for goat's shin stew.'

He poured two large glasses of Barolo, and some Evian water for Greg, who immediately impressed him by announcing, 'Evian is naïve backwards!' Clare smiled happily at her bright son, and Andy realized that, after years of self-denial and deprivation, his wife had been revivified. Her eyes were shining, her skin had a fresh lustre — even her hair seemed to have acquired an added sheen.

She drank some wine and said, 'Even before he won the Lottery, I thought of Brad as the man who won. He had his own firm, the biggest house, the best car.'

'And now?'

'And now I can see that the man who won is a different person altogether. Thank God I went into the bookshop that afternoon.'

Andy felt triumphant as she said this, but the triumph, long awaited, was blurred. It wasn't quite the uninhibited surge of joy he expected. As he drank the wine he tried to picture Clive, waiting alone and probably bored in his dreary London flat, and Brad sharing a fetid cell with an arsonist or a mugger, and he wondered sadly why fate had decided to destroy the happy families dream that Brad had thought his money could create.

We do hope that you have enjoyed reading this large print book.

Did you know that all of our titles are available for purchase?

We publish a wide range of high quality large print books including:
Romances, Mysteries, Classics
General Fiction
Non Fiction and Westerns

Special interest titles available in large print are:
The Little Oxford Dictionary
Music Book
Song Book
Hymn Book
Service Book

Also available from us courtesy of Oxford University Press:
Young Readers' Dictionary
(large print edition)
Young Readers' Thesaurus
(large print edition)

For further information or a free brochure, please contact us at:
Ulverscroft Large Print Books Ltd.,
The Green, Bradgate Road, Anstey,
Leicester, LE7 7FU, England.
Tel: (00 44) 0116 236 4325
Fax: (00 44) 0116 234 0205

Other titles published by
The House of Ulverscroft:

THE VALLEY

Barry Pilton

It is the 1980s and in mid-Wales the inhabitants of the Nant Valley are holding out against the modern world. Then outsiders discover the valley, and wrongly believe it to be an idyll. Mysterious Stéfan buys a derelict manor house and sets about becoming a squire. Jane and Rob, poor arty urbanites with an enthusiasm for alfresco nudity, buy a tumbledown farmhouse. Meanwhile, Dafydd the postman doubts the valley is ready for outsiders — and as they struggle with sexual scandal, hostile artisans and a corpse, the omens are not good.

THE WIFE

Meg Wolitzer

Joe and Joan Castleman are en route to Helsinki. Joe is thinking about the prestigious literary prize he will receive and Joan is plotting how to leave him. For too long Joan has played the role of supportive wife, turning a blind eye to his misdemeanours, subjugating her own talents and quietly being the keystone of his success ... This is an acerbic and astonishing take on a marriage and the truth that behind the compromises, dedication and promise inherent in marriage there so often lies a secret ...

GRABBING THE FAMILY JEWELS

Gaby Hauptmann

Anno Adelmann — survivor of two heart attacks — is a wealthy widower, and his four scheming daughters all have designs on his inheritance. Anno, who refers to them variously as hyenas and piranhas, decides to have a bit of fun at their expense. But what starts as a joke soon becomes much more serious, and the family finds itself dealing with kidnapping, blackmail and even attempted murder. Vanity is mocked and bad behaviour deliciously punished as the four sisters learn some uncomfortable lessons in sibling rivalry.

BILBURY PIE

Vernon Coleman

Bilbury is a small village nestling on the edge of Exmoor in North Devon which is home to a wonderful array of colourful characters. Bilbury is the sort of traditional village which offers a way of life so often envied by town and city dwellers. It boasts a warm and welcoming village pub, crackling log fires, home-made bread, vegetables fresh from the garden and cricket on the village green. This collection of short stories features many of the regular characters from the Bilbury series of novels — and also introduces one or two new faces as well.

THE ARTIST OF EIKANDO

Linda Lee Welch

Junko Bayliss is a potter, famous for her exquisite designs. From the outside, she is seen as a successful, independent artist, but from the inside, Junko knows that her personal life is a mess. When her elegant but emotionally cold parents die only a few minutes apart, Junko is left to ponder the question marks that always hovered over her parents' lives, and their strange behaviour towards their only child. When her Aunt Helen hints at a mystery — something shocking that happened to Diane and Peter Bayliss during the Second World War — Junko decides to visit Japan, where her parents met, and hunt out their story . . .